THE ARIS EFFECT

Also by Rae Lamar

Unlike Me

Somewhere In Between

Open

22

Dawn of Aris

THE ARIS EFFECT

a novel by:

Rae Lamar

STOCK PHOTOGRAPHY: iStockphoto LP

COVER DESIGN: Rae Lamar

PUBLISHED BY: Rae Lamar

PRINTED IN THE UNITED STATES OF AMERICA

ISBN 978-0-9972119-0-0

~ 1 ~

AUGUST

"Moody."

When Aris didn't respond to him, Luke shifted his gaze from the flat panel television to her silk-wrapped head resting heavily against his chest. It was eight in the morning. Way too early for what he had in mind, but he tried it anyway.

Dropping his hand, he rubbed her ass.

She didn't move. Not that he expected her to.

"Moody," Luke said again as he trailed a finger along her spine.

Nothing.

Grinning, he lowered his left hand to rest on the dangerous curve of her hip. Those playful disruptions rarely woke Aris but were usually enough to incite her to receive him. And though burying himself deep inside of her walls was very much on his mind at the moment, that wasn't Luke's primary goal.

He was hungry.

They had done room service the past three mornings, but Luke wanted to venture out for breakfast and get back before the heat peaked. Why Aris wanted to experience Vegas for the first time in August was still a puzzle to him, especially when she complained about the blazing sun every time they stepped foot on the Strip. He'd tried to explain the concept of a desert hell to her two months ago, but Aris insisted that the suffocating humidity they endured living in Atlanta was much worse.

"Whatever, Donovan," she'd said with a flip of her hand. "Dry heat is doable!"

That was partially correct but, instead of trying to convince Aris to postpone their mini-vacation until the autumn season, Luke decided that he would let her feel the truth of a Sin City summer for herself.

While absently stroking her hip, he silently debated whether or not it was worth it to wake her. He'd been propped on pillows and flipping channels for about an hour, and it hadn't bothered Aris at all. She simply shifted with him, twisting her long limbs around him without fully rousing from her deep slumber. It was what she often did whenever he tossed or turned in bed, unconsciously seeking him out until she was practically attached to his side once more.

But as sweet as she could be during the night, the rising sun always brought a different reality.

In the three months since Aris had been spending every weekend and some weeknights with him at his apartment, Luke had quickly learned that "Aris In The

Morning" was a stressful experience and it was best to make sure that they never had a purpose before 10AM. Which was why he was now considering that it would be better to wait until she began stirring on her own in a couple of hours...

But the vivid vision of them enjoying a champagne breakfast at some fancy spot with a spectacular view was beginning to provoke second and third thoughts that eventually triggered Luke's stomach to growl audibly in famished approval of the feast in his mind.

"Dude," Aris mumbled, finally lifting her head to glare at him through tired eyes. "That was my ear."

He kissed the wrinkle between her brows and gently guided her head back to his chest.

His internal debate was settled.

A champagne *brunch* would have to do.

Aris began to stir.

Four moans. Six sighs.

When she lifted her head to look at him this time, Luke was greeted with a wicked grin.

He laughed. "I'll handle that *after* we eat, woman."

She pinned him with another glare.

But her grin stayed in place.

Aris followed Luke into the glass-enclosed shower where he eventually succumbed to her suggestive moans and sighs, giving her what she needed against the tiled wall. Since their arrival a few days ago, Aris had been in rare form which was an occasional phenomenon that Luke quickly learned to enjoy when it surfaced, resulting in voracious, erotic spurts that were as bizarre as her random cycles of restlessness and hibernation.

It wasn't long before they were exquisitely drained, exchanging lazy kisses and unnecessary caresses as they slowly lathered each other with soap and eager hands. When Luke leaned in for round two, Aris laughed and reminded him of his growling stomach, forcing him out of the shower. She remained under the spray and asked Luke to find the travel-sized bottles of shampoo and conditioner in her toiletry bag, her reasoning being that her hair was already wet so she may as well wash it too. Of course, that caused further delay once she stepped out of the shower and proceeded to attack the tangled strands with the complimentary hair dryer before wrestling it into submission first with a flat iron and then with a curling wand. She'd taken no more than about forty minutes, eventually choosing to pile her hair on top of her head in a messy ponytail, coyly apologizing that she'd taken so long when he was so hungry. Grinning, Luke kissed her forehead, completely entertained just watching her, realizing that it was yet another reason why he loved her so much. He would have gladly canceled brunch to schedule an appointment at the hotel salon if she wanted; instead, Aris waved off the idea and handled the task herself. Her simplicity was as refreshing as how impossibly cute she now looked dashing out of their hotel room, leaving him and her signature flirty, cheerful scent in her wake.

Luckily, they arrived at the swanky restaurant in

time. From the panoramic view to the fantastic food, it turned out to be the best boozy brunch ever.

Buzzing off several mimosas, Aris toasted to good times and multimillion-dollar jackpots before rushing Luke to pay the bill so she could try her luck at the slots. They ducked in and out of a few vintage Vegas resorts on the northern edge of the strip, racking up modest payouts until the blistering heat won and they caught a cab to head back south to their hotel.

"What now?" Luke asked as they strolled through the crowded lobby, side-stepping the swarm of overly-eager tourists scrambling toward the boxing ring to take selfies with the Golden Lion.

"Let's go back to the room and chill for a while." Aris looked up at him, uncertainty in her eyes. "Is that okay with you?"

"Anywhere with you is okay with me."

Her face lit up and Luke smiled. As corny as his admission sounded to his own ears, he meant every word. Luke had yet to tire of her or become bored, no matter what they did together, and he was beginning to believe that maybe, just maybe…he never would.

They retreated to their room for a few hours and ordered snacks and desserts from room service along with a pay-per-view movie. They didn't speak one word, completely satisfied just being in each other's space. It was one of the many things Luke loved most about her. With Aris, he didn't have to be *on* all the time. There were never any blatant or even subtle expectations from her to fill every minute of their free time with tasks and people. For the first time in what felt like forever, Luke could actually take a vacation and just…*be.*

Given how incredibly rare that was just one year ago, Luke grinned and dropped his head to inhale the freshly-washed scent of Aris's hair. He pulled her closer to him now and inhaled again, the reality of his new life with her causing his heart to swell.

"You okay?" she asked absently, still engrossed in the movie he'd long ago stopped watching because Aris was way more entertaining.

"I'm okay, baby."

"You need me?"

Luke smiled at that, appreciating how she was always so aware of him. "I always need you…but I'm good. This is perfect."

Aris accepted his answer with a simple nod. Her eyes were trained on the television, but she still leaned forward and wiggled her ass against his crotch to let him know that he was full of shit and she knew the truth. Laughing, he waited until she settled against him before his lips found her ear to reassure her that, despite his severely-aroused condition, he really was satisfied with just holding her.

"I've got a surprise for you," Luke finally said after the movie credits rolled.

Aris stiffened in his arms.

"Yeah, yeah. You hate surprises. Okay, bad choice of words." He paused as she turned to pin him with a questioning stare. "Just get up and get dressed. You're gonna love it."

And she did.

Knowing how much Aris adored The King of Pop, Luke secured amazing seats to MJ One at Mandalay

Bay weeks ago. The minute they entered the theater, she began wiggling her hips and bopping around in excitement. After taking dozens of pictures inside the lobby in front of the superstar's iconic sequined-jacket-black-Fedora *Billie Jean* image, they continued into the theater to sit and enjoy the pre-show entertainment. When the lights finally dimmed and the stage came to life, there was no longer a wonder why it was considered the best show on the Strip. Aris was in awe as the stellar cast performed a series of hits including *Thriller*, which instantly conjured memories in her mind of the first time she saw the groundbreaking video as a bright-eyed kid and somehow grasped without question what she was meant to do for the rest of her life.

For Aris, the spectacular production was an acute, emotional reminder that delivered perfect peace to her soul, a serenity so profound that, halfway through the performance, she tore her misty eyes away from the magic to stare lovingly at Luke, who simply smiled his complete understanding and kissed her forehead.

"Thank you sooo much, baby," Aris gushed as they exited the theater arm-in-arm two hours later. She was on a natural high, singing songs from the show during their short cab ride back to the hotel, through the lobby of their hotel and on the elevator as they rapidly ascended to the twenty-seventh floor. Luke exited after Aris and her voice trailed off as they walked hand-in-hand down the dimly-lit hallway to their suite. Once inside, Aris was out of her dress in seconds.

"Tonight was incredible," she said, tugging at Luke's belt after he let the door slam shut. Reaching inside his boxers, Aris wrapped her hand around the thick, rigid length of him that had been teasing her all afternoon. "I'm still not a fan of surprises, Donovan...but I absolutely love you."

"Is that right?" Pleased by the sudden shift and rapid emergence of her insatiable nature, Luke secured the privacy latch on the heavy door and lifted Aris off her feet, carrying her into the bedroom as she eagerly trailed kisses down his neck. "Show me."

~ 2 ~

"I eat plums in summer."

Aris's words lingered in the air as she continued to poke the mixture of salad greens in her bowl with a shiny fork, fully appreciating the artistry of it all but really wishing it would magically transform into a plate of tacos.

Luke tapped his leg against hers underneath the table causing Aris to look up and glance at him. He raised a brow, the amusement in his eyes contradicting the serious look on his face. Her bratty behavior and flippant quips weren't doing him any favors at the moment so Aris straightened in her chair and leaned forward, ready to deliver the more appropriate response that she had agreed to share when presented with the always-pretentious, *"so...what do you do?"* question that perfect strangers always ask each other for lack of more worthwhile conversation.

"I'm a make-up artist."

More silence followed as the men at the table drew blank expressions while their wives seemed to silently assess the fact that outside of several strokes of mascara on her lashes and a few swipes of gloss across her lips, there wasn't a drop of makeup on Aris's fresh, flawless face.

"How...interesting," Georgine Harris finally uttered with a pleasant smile. "Brides and models, I presume?"

"Ghouls and zombies, mostly," Aris replied, sweetly. "Though I guess they're all pretty much one and the same these days...wouldn't you say?"

Georgine pressed her lips together in disapproval as her husband, Bart, and a few of the other men at the table released amused chuckles masked as hearty grunts. Aris felt another tap underneath the table and she risked another glance at Luke. He didn't look her way this time, but his mouth twitched. Lifting his glass from the table, Luke took a long sip of water to hide his grin then lifted a dark linen napkin from his lap, swiped it across his mouth, relaxed his posture and expertly changed the subject.

As the group began yet another conversation that was above Aris's pay-grade, she felt Luke's hand on her thigh. He knew she hated suffering these boring business dinners as much as he did, but it was a necessary evil in his line of work. They would be on their way back to their hotel soon enough so Aris conjured up her most genuine smile and listened quietly as Luke engaged the other dinner guests in more stuffy conversation...and inched his hand up her thigh. Basically, his slick way of reminding her that—if she endured this for him just a while longer—there would be fun times ahead.

Spreading her legs slightly to give Luke better access, Aris accepted his challenge and widened her smile.

She really had no reason to complain. The majority of their vacation so far had been work-free and would have remained that way had Devin not called right before noon to tell Luke that there were some potential clients who happened to be in Vegas and wanted to meet before flying out the next morning. Aris hadn't even been mad when Luke rose from their table for two and left her to eat lunch alone for twenty minutes while he talked shop with Devin.

Of course work would happen...eventually.

But her whole plan for their vacation had been to save Luke from boring-ass meetings and conference calls while they played in the desert. Some fun and excitement was just what they both needed, not to mention some extended time alone. With Aris's late-night shoots and Luke's constant travel, all they ever had time for were occasional calls, video chats and dirty texts and lately they felt grateful for the opportunity to spend more than twenty-four hours of quality time with each other.

Their schedules were hell and not at all conducive to their slightly-new relationship but, despite that major personal inconvenience, Aris was ecstatic about her professional progress. Not only was she working on the set of one of the hottest horror drama shows on television, but she had also been networking her ass off and making serious connections resulting in side gigs and additional projects that were helping to solidify her rising credibility within the industry.

Aris had come a long way since palling around with her CDMI crew in Los Angeles. Soon after beginning her first gig in Atlanta, she built solid relationships with at least a dozen members of the production crew but it was ultimately with Troy and Nate that Aris experienced the most genuine connection. She later introduced them to Kyle, her friend from her college days and a pretty sought-after photographer who still lived in the metro area after they graduated. It was Kyle who kept them in the loop about local events and exposed them to contracts that existed under the radar within his vast network, resulting in premier projects, memorable work and extra income for them all.

Aris took a sip of water and beamed, feeling ten feet tall on the inside. It was pretty amazing how far she'd come. This time last year, she was finishing school and pondering what was next for her life.

Today, her life was surreal.

Complete with a dream job and a dream man.

Aris couldn't remember ever feeling this content, despite how much she and Luke had transformed into two workaholics passing in the night...which was why Aris had intended for this Vegas trip to be an escape though she was quickly realizing that, especially for Luke, escaping work was a joke and there was definitely no such thing as down time.

Ergo, this dry-ass business dinner conversation.

After suffering another hour, Aris was relieved when the other couples decided to turn in early for the night. Luke and Aris said their goodbyes and decided to forgo the cab ride and stroll down the strip to their hotel, stopping ever so often to enjoy the sights and beautiful night.

As soon Luke pushed the door of their suite open, Aris took off for the small kitchen.

"I'm starving!"

Observing her, Luke loosened his tie. "What are you about to mess up? You and that microwave have not been friends. Maybe you should just do room service."

"Whatever," Aris replied, flipping her hand. True, she'd ruined some leftovers the other night, heating up a plate of pasta into a shriveled, rubbery mess but that was then. She was certain the evil microwave would be kind to the Pad Thai Luke never finished thanks to Devin's interruption of their late lunch. "Bet it'll still be better than the weeds and tree bark we had for dinner." She turned away to reach into the refrigerator. "You know you want some…"

Straightening to her enhanced height from the four-inched heels on her feet, Aris stepped back and collided with Luke's solid frame as she closed the door.

"Damn right," he said, his voice rumbling in her ear, sending jolts through her body. "I do."

Luke's lips found her nape as his right hand fumbled with the side zipper of her dress while the other teased her taut nipple through the thin material. Aris bit her lip in response to the stimulation, still amazed by her natural, effortless reaction to him. No matter where they were — morning, noon or night — all he ever had to do was put his lips and hands in the right spot and sex was a foregone conclusion.

Every. Single. Time.

After several playful minutes, Luke had Aris on the

edge of the counter, stripped her of everything except her heels and jewelry. She gasped the moment he filled her, moaned as he stroked her fast and deep, his mouth moving from her neck to her ear as he whispered everything he intended to do to her before they made it to the bed.

Closing her eyes, Aris held on as Luke continued rewarding her for a worthy showing and good behavior at that dry-ass business dinner, a small smile touching her lips until Luke hit her spot, forcing a gasp and several melodic moans to escape her mouth.

Fun times, indeed.

When Aris and Luke woke the next morning, they agreed to go all out and make the most of their final day and night in Vegas. Luke knew better than to comment on the ease with which Aris was able to hop out of bed and be dressed by 9AM, but he realized that lounging by the pool definitely had something to do with her uncharacteristic, early morning cooperation.

Adorned in a colorful bikini and netted cover up, Aris rushed Luke down to the massive outdoor complex for a refreshing dip and some relaxation, but their growling stomachs forced them to take a quick detour to *Blizz* and grab some crepes, smoothies and deliciously-decorated yogurt to satisfy their hunger from the previous night of lust and love.

"At least it's not a thousand degrees this morning," Aris said thirty minutes later, settling onto her lounge chair next to him after returning from floating down the winding lazy river. "I'm so glad we came. Wish we could stay."

"Yeah," Luke replied absently, scrolling through his phone. He felt Aris's eyes on him, and he smiled sheepishly at her silent reprimand. "I'm almost done."

"Work, work, work," she muttered, shaking her head. "What does a girl have to do to get you relax?"

Lifting his head, Luke leaned over to kiss her. "You're doing it, baby. I haven't been this relaxed in..." His gaze dropped to consider it. "Shit. *Ever.*"

Satisfied with his answer, Aris accepted another extended kiss before reclining in her lounge chair. Just as she was about to ask Luke what was so urgent back at the office, her phone buzzed. Luke cut his eyes at her with an intuitive nod as she grabbed it to check her notifications. When Aris gave him a silly smile to acknowledge he was indeed correct that it was work-related, Luke grinned and went back to tapping his own screen.

"Whatever," she said. "This is like the first issue I've received since we've been here, so I *still* won."

Placing his phone on the small table on his left side, Luke leaned back in the lounger and glanced to his right to give Aris another knowing nod before he relaxed and closed his eyes. She stuck her tongue out at him, and he laughed. "I saw that."

She laughed along with him as she read and replied to her message. A few minutes later, she put her phone away. "It's Kyle. He has a photo shoot with Tarrah and Marcie next Thursday. Shouldn't take too long, so I told him I'd do it. You want to come?"

"I won't be back until Friday afternoon, baby. I'm meeting Devin in St. Louis to close a client."

"Oh. Forgot." She picked at her nails. "Do you think things will be slowing down for you anytime soon?"

"Hard to tell, but to be honest, I hope not. We're way ahead of our original projections and if we keep this up, we'll be pulling national clients in no time."

Aris smiled. "No shit?"

"Real shit." Luke opened his eyes and lifted his arm to run a hand back and forth over his head. A small smile teased his lips. "It's crazy right now."

"Crazy? It's fan-freaking-tastic!" She threw her arms high in the air. "You're about to blooowww uuuppp!"

"Goofy ass," he replied in jest as he grabbed his shades and slipped them over his eyes. "Come here."

"Come where?" She raised a brow. "That thing isn't big enough for the both of us."

Luke's silence served as his disagreement with her assessment. Pressing her lips together, Aris shifted to his lounger, aligning her body next to his until she fit perfectly against him.

"Oh." She nodded in approval. "You be knowin'."

He guided her head to his chest, saying nothing.

They remained that way, no words and twisted limbs, relaxing…until the sun won again. It was almost noon when they arrived back in their suite to change and head back down to the casino to play the slots for a little while before taking the monorail to the other resorts. By late afternoon, the two found themselves back in bed, making lazy love until they fell asleep. The alarm Luke set on his phone sounded off at 8PM and they hopped up to shower and dress again for a night out. Dinner was another amazing experience followed by rounds and rounds of shots. Stumbling from the restaurant, Aris took charge of the rest of their night, rushing Luke from one rooftop bar to the next. When they arrived at their final destination atop a replica of the Eiffel Tower, she paused to look out at the amazing view of the water show and bright lights of the legendary Vegas Strip.

Moving to stand behind her, Luke gripped Aris's waist and kissed her bare shoulder before nuzzling his face into the slight curve of her neck. It was the first time in hours that they had stopped to take it all in, to truly appreciate the night and each other.

"My mother loved Paris," she said quietly, staring at the dancing fountains. "My Dad said it was her favorite city on her earth. It's where I was conceived, the place I was named after...well, sort of." Turning in his arms, she stared at him, her eyes shining. "Thank you for bringing me here. I love you."

Before Luke could respond, Aris pressed her lips against his. It was light and feathery at first and Luke let Aris set the pace, sensing her vulnerability in that moment. First, her hands caressed his face then shifted to lightly graze the back of his head with her nails, making him throb, but still he remained passive, enjoying the explorative way she was tasting him, touching him...breathing him in. Slipping her tongue in his mouth, she tangled with him until he finally took over and matched her hypnotic rhythm, forcing the sweetest moan to escape her lips as she grinded her body against him.

Completely enthralled by Aris's blatant displays of

affection, Luke reluctantly remembered where they were and reached up to stroke her neck with his hand, the slow movements an almost futile effort to calm the storm he knew was raging within her, one he intended to savor once they'd made it back to the privacy of their suite.

But now was not the time.

Aris's eyes fluttered opened and she graced him with passioned eyes and a hint of a smile, that same look he'd seen every night of their too-short vacation. Luke adored that peaceful expression, so much that he risked one last, prolonged kiss before he forced himself to pull back, careful not to put on another show for passersby and possibly get them escorted out.

Sighing, Aris allowed Luke to turn her attention towards the water show. She leaned her head and body back against his solid frame.

Luke smiled and rested the top of his chin on her head, securing her in his arms. "I love you too."

"Oh Gaaawwwddd…"

Aris placed a hand over her mouth and waited for the nausea to subside.

It didn't.

Untangling herself from Luke's naked, sleeping body and jumping frantically from the bed, Aris stumbled her way to the bathroom as quickly as she could.

Dropping to her knees, she positioned herself over the toilet and waited.

And waited.

And finally sat her ass on the toilet.

She relieved herself for what seemed like forever and when the steady stream lessened to a trickle and then to nothing at all, she continued to sit because she was too tired to stand.

When she heard Luke stir and call her name in concern, Aris grabbed some tissue, handled her business and finally stood...only to grimace as little prickly needles spread throughout her legs causing her to limp to the sink.

"I'm fine...go back to sleep."

After washing and drying her hands, she glanced into the wide mirror in front her, noticing the faint mark on her neck and the sparkle in her eyes thanks to Luke. Aris stared at her reflection, trying to remember specific details from last night night, but the only thing that wasn't fuzzy in her mind was when she kissed Luke at the top of the Eiffel Tower. She smiled to herself, thinking that if somehow that was the only memory she would have of their night together, she was certain that it had been the very best part.

Exiting the bathroom, Aris wandered out of the bedroom and continued into the living area of their suite on her way to the kitchenette. Her mouth was dry as hell, so she opened the fridge and snatched one of the bottles of water. It probably cost twenty bucks or something crazy, but she opened it anyway and drank almost half the bottle before stopping to take a breath.

Leaning against the counter, she slowly sipped the rest of it as her eyes darted around the suite. They would be heading home soon, and the thought instantly saddened her. Her happiest moments were when she and Luke were alone, just living and laughing and loving. Returning home would interrupt all of that, reinstating the busy schedules that their jobs demanded along with the subsequent distance.

Pushing away from the counter, Aris turned and noticed some loose papers on the end table in the other room near the sofa. She walked over to sift through the small pile, suddenly deciding that she and Luke would have to find a way to get away more often.

They needed it. She needed it.

Her mind began to race with possibilities.

Maybe they could go to New York City? She'd never been there either. After that, they could do Bermuda and then the Bahamas and Cancun and—

What the fuck?

Letting the others fall from her hands to the carpeted floor, Aris gripped and stared at the remaining paper in her hand, a questionably-designed document with a prominent logo in the top corner that made her eyes widen. She read every word on the page and raced into the bedroom to shake and push Luke, who sat up quickly once his mind registered the panic in her voice. When she thrust the paper in his face, Luke rubbed his eyes lazily and scanned it quickly. Aris waited for a reaction, surprised when it turned out to be the complete opposite of her own.

"Yeah," he finally said, tossing the paper onto the nightstand. "I peeped that when I was up earlier. It's nothing, baby. Come here." Pulling her down into the bed, Luke secured her against his body as his mouth kissed and teased her neck. "I need you."

Aris lay there for only a moment before she began to kick and push her way out of his stronghold to stand next to the bed, still unnerved by what she'd read. Once she was able to find her words, Aris's questions tumbled out in rapid succession until Luke grabbed her hand and slowly stroked the inside of her palm with his thumb.

"Moody, calm down…"

Aris stopped her inquisition only to stare down at Luke in amazement, curious as to why he seemed so calm and indifferent.

An observation became her very next question.

"Because it's not a big deal, baby" he answered, still stroking her palm. "Right now, all I care about is you helping me get rid of this headache…which was what I was trying to do before you kicked the shit out of me."

Luke's eyes dropped from her face to her nipples peeking through the thin material of her tee. Reaching up, he teased both with his hands, causing Aris to chew on her lip until her mind let go of the contents of the document on the nightstand and focused solely on the sensations Luke was building within her.

"Relax," he whispered, pulling her into bed until she was on her back and he was hovering over her. "Clearly we were beyond wasted to have scheduled to elope the day after tomorrow knowing we're heading back home this afternoon." He shifted, spreading her legs as he maneuvered his body so his head was near the apex of her thighs. When he was properly positioned, he caught her eyes. "You're thinking too much, baby. Everything is fine. Nothing happened." Running a finger slowly over her swollen clit, his eyes darkened. "But would it have been so bad if it had?"

Aris tilted her head in shock, and he released an amused breath that tickled her swollen folds. She gasped as his fingers went to work again, closing her eyes as desire flooded her core.

"I love you, Aris. And I would be lying if I told you that the thought of you being mine and of us being married...the thought of you being *my wife*...didn't make me smile."

Aris could no longer focus or respond as Luke continued to slowly stroke her with his fingers...then his tongue...then his dick...her mind letting go of every worry to enjoy every single thing he was doing to her body for the next half hour.

Exhausted, Aris avoided Luke's eyes and settled her head against his chest. Her legs naturally snaked their way through his and she tried but failed to relax, too preoccupied with over-analyzing his confession and contemplating how she should react to him feeling so sure about wanting a real future...with *her*.

Her mind was reeling.

Not because she wasn't in love with him — she was.

Undeniably. Completely.

Still, her angst was real.

Because the sudden idea of marriage and the possible, impossible reality of one day becoming Mrs. Luke Donovan was, in her mind, the equivalent of a seismic shift in the newly-poured foundation of their relationship, one that would bring about a level of intimacy that Aris was undeniably certain that she would completely *fuck up*.

~ 3 ~

"You're in a place."

Aris glanced at Luke. Blinked. "Nope."

"Moody..."

She turned her head to look out the window.

Luke kept driving, debating whether or not he should let her work through this funk she'd been in since they checked out of the resort. Aris was disturbingly quiet the entire flight to Atlanta and, though he wanted to probe, he gave her space. If Luke knew nothing else, he understood that she would talk when she was ready and not a moment sooner.

But that was hours ago.

Now, he felt that it was time to dispel her mounting distress and try to alleviate the destructive thoughts she'd probably been wrestling with since she spotting the document that itemized their botched, drunken attempt at a premature happily ever after.

"Do me a favor?"

Aris twisted her hands in her lap before nodding for him to continue.

"Stop thinking." Luke slowed the car to a stop at the red light and waited until Aris looked at him before he spoke again. "We were drunk off our asses last night and obviously not in our right minds. But the reality is...nothing happened. We are still us. We are not married. But clearly there's a deep, sober part of both of us that genuinely loves each other enough to have ended up wanting to marry at all. At least, that's what I choose to believe. Still, that's *all* it was, baby...a stupid stunt by two completely lit, crazy-in-love people...a wild-ass memory and a you-remember-when story for us to tell at house parties and cookouts one day. Nothing more, nothing less. Okay?"

She took a deep breath. "Okay."

"Say it with your chest."

Aris playfully slapped Luke's arm and he grinned, happy to see her finally let it all go.

Or so he hoped.

Luke could reasonably understand Aris's panic, but what he couldn't figure out was why her anxiety about what they'd almost done hadn't faded yet... especially considering that the only consequence of their foolish actions last night had been losing the $99 deposit for the ceremony. While Aris was in the shower, Luke had pulled out his phone and searched the internet for the company name he recalled from the top of the invoice. Reading the details of their wedding package online, Luke stifled a laugh. Even now, he had to shake his head at the thought of them getting married in an actual drive-thru ceremony with a car embellished with the tagline, "Putting Matrimony In Motion."

What the hell had they been wasted on to think *that* was the move?

After pulling to a stop in the short driveway of his townhouse-style apartment, Luke cut the engine. He unloaded the car and followed Aris to the front door where she slipped her key into the lock to let them inside. When she took off for the bedroom, Luke went back out to retrieve the mail from the past week. There was quite a bit of it so, instead of dropping it on the coffee table, Luke sorted and opened most of it before returning to joining Aris upstairs.

He walked into the master bathroom just as Aris opened the shower door and stepped out, leaving the water running as she watched him undress. Reaching for the handle, he was surprised to see she'd already adjusted the water for him. Looking up to tell her so, Luke found her staring at him with an adorable smirk on her face as she wrapped herself in a towel. His body instantly reacted to the stunning sight as he stepped inside, his eyes following her until she disappeared into the bedroom where he would bet money that she would stretch out on top of the bed to air dry and search for something good on television.

Luke shook his head and smiled.

Adjusting the water to a human temperature…check.

Dripping water on the comforter…work in progress.

Finishing up his shower, Luke stepped out and grabbed a towel to dry off before padding naked to the bed where Aris was already nodding off. Pulling her to her feet, he removed the towel from her body and used it to finish drying her off. She rubbed her eyes and yawned while he stepped away to hang her damp towel on the hook in the bathroom next to his and grab a silk scarf from the counter, which he extended to her before getting in bed. After tying up her hair, Aris turned off the television and turned to Luke, twisting her limbs around him and snuggling as close as she could possibly get.

Luke woke first.

He didn't move, choosing to lie quietly and mentally review his upcoming tasks and meetings for the week, holding Aris until she started stirring and finally opened her eyes a half hour later. She reached for the remote and brought the television to life, settling on an old Marvel movie after Luke nodded his approval. They remained that way, tangled and cozy, until the home phone rang around noon.

Rolling her eyes, Aris groaned.

One glance at the caller ID and she snatched the cordless device from the nightstand, promptly passing it to Luke without answering. He accepted the phone and pressed TALK, already clear by Aris's actions who the caller was on the other end of the line.

"Celeste," he greeted, warmly. "How are you?"

Aris heard her stepmother's voice through the earpiece but didn't bother to make out what she was saying. After a few minutes of pleasant chit-chat, Luke told Celeste that they would see her soon, producing more eye rolls from Aris. When he suddenly laughed at something else Celeste said, she lifted her head and glared at him as he disconnected the call.

"What's so funny?"

Luke kissed her nose. "You."

Before she could protest, he shut her up with sex.

Afterwards, they showered together and rushed to get dressed so they wouldn't be late for Celeste's Sunday dinner at her house in Macon...which happened to be her father's house as well, now that he and Celeste were totally married and sharing stuff and property too.

Not that Aris was expecting them to get divorced right after their wedding or anything. It was more that she hadn't believed...well, she wasn't quite sure what she believed but she did know that it was completely bizarre to have an actual stepmother who liked to cook and bake on Sundays and have her kids over after church like a real-life Publix commercial. And since Celeste was never able to have children of her own...

Tag.

Aris was it.

With Luke in tow by default.

It was only once a month, sometimes twice when Tony and Celeste's calendars permitted. They still lived full-time in Savannah and, while Tony was retired, Celeste still worked a consultant's schedule for an accounting firm in Macon. It was where she lived before meeting Tony Collier one weekend during a conference she was attending in Savannah. Celeste had arrived a few days early to take advantage of the historic city and perfect weather. "It was destined,"

Celeste always cooed when telling the story of her nine-month whirlwind love affair with Tony and how traveling up and down the interstate eventually got the best of them.

Their solution?

Marriage and dual residences.

And, for now, they seemed to be living the picket fence dream complete with convenient Sunday dinners in Macon, so Aris wouldn't have an excuse to cancel because they were meeting her and Luke halfway.

When they arrived, Aris and Luke walked hand-in-hand to the front door. The ranch-style house was picture perfect with immaculate landscaping and a wraparound porch. It was deceivingly large as it also had a finished, walk-out basement that was basically another house itself.

Aris thought back to the first time she and Luke visited. From the curb, it was a nice enough house but, once inside, the floor plan and the sheer size of the place caught her completely by surprise. By the time she and Luke were ready to get on the road back to Atlanta, Aris had actually become quite fond of her father and his wife's second home.

But not enough to be there every other week.

Celeste opened the door and smiled brightly before Luke could press the doorbell, extending her arms wide in a silent request for a hug. Luke indulged her and quickly stepped aside so Aris could get some of the love too. As Celeste embraced her, a delicious aroma wafted through the doorway to her nose and Aris stood stiffly, anticipating today's delicious menu.

Because Celeste cooked her ass off.

Grudgingly, Aris had become quite fond of that too.

Entering the house, she greeted Tony with a warm smile and a kiss on his stubbly cheek. Her father appeared almost as lost she was, which helped Aris to relax that much more. She was pretty sure that this bi-monthly Sunday family dinner was Celeste's and Luke's master plan to get Aris to bond more with Tony and trigger their transformation into a real family.

The guest list was always the same.

Tony, Celeste, Luke and Aris.

Some Sundays, they would just watch a movie after dinner. Other times, they would play cards or board games. Tony would break out all his old records — yes, records — and prattle on and on about "when music was real music." Aris had to admit that her father's collection was impressive. Tony Collier loved music with every fiber of his being, and Aris was pretty sure that it was her deceased mother, Lydia, who had everything to do with that truth.

This Sunday, however, was more low key.

Maybe it was because Tony and Celeste sensed that Aris and Luke were tired from their vacation or maybe it was because they had all become comfortable enough with each other to not have to feel the need to entertain or be entertained the entire visit. Either way, Aris was grateful for the reprieve from the extended games and invasive conversation after dinner and chose to take complete advantage of it.

She wandered out onto the porch alone just as the sun was setting. Even with the comfortable silence in the house, Aris still needed to get away and have a minute to herself. At times, it all became a bit too much for her, all the bonding that was so important to Celeste and Luke. Aris knew their hearts were in the right place, but it still felt like so much pressure. Tony always played along too, much in the half-hearted way that she did; their genuine attempt to appease the ones they loved and who loved them both enough to arrange it all.

Scanning the picturesque street, Aris heard the front door swing open and then close with a snap.

Tony stepped out onto the porch and settled next to her on the top step of the concrete stairs that led to the lawn. He extended a healthy plate of apple cobbler, one that matched the serving he had in his other hand. Aris thanked him and accepted it with a small smile. Not because she was hungry but because she knew that he was simply trying to do just what their significant others wanted them to do—bond.

"You're welcome," he said, passing her a silver, plastic fork. "It's fresh out of the oven."

"Looks yummy." She glanced at him after eating two bites. It was delicious, of course...because Celeste made it from scratch. "Why aren't you eating?"

Tony laughed, emitting a deep rumble from his gut. "Just taking a break. I've already had two plates of it. She outdid herself this time. I swear that woman's mission in life is to keep me fat and happy."

Aris grinned at her father. "There are worse things."

Tony eventually began nibbling his cobbler as Aris finished hers. They sat together, enjoying Celeste's masterful baking, in silence.

"So how's work?" Tony finally asked.

"Super busy." Aris sat her empty plate on the step

below her. "Crazy hours, but I really love what I'm doing. And I've also been doing more side work, you know…to get my name out there."

"That's great," Tony replied, looking directly at Aris for the first time since he'd joined her on the porch. "I'm proud of you."

Aris sat up straighter and beamed. "Thanks, Dad."

Tony chuckled and turned his head to glance across the street at nothing. "One thing's for sure…you didn't get any of that from me."

"Definitely not," Aris said, laughing with him.

"That's your mother in you," he added with a nod. "All that creativity and fire and passion for what you do. She was just like that. Like you."

"And you hate it."

Aris hadn't meant to say that out loud, to ruin the progress they were making in that moment. Tony didn't have to bring apple cobbler and sit with her. He didn't have to try, but he did. Yet, it somehow felt wrong not to acknowledge the elephant in the room, not to speak the truth.

"I don't hate that about you, and I never hated it about your mother," Tony clarified. "Back then, I just didn't always understand it. Or her. I loved your mother so much it scared me. I can admit that now."

Three cars traveled down the wide, tree-lined street, the last one in succession almost rear-ending the Toyota as the primary mini-van suddenly slowed to allow a little boy to run out and retrieve his basketball. Behind the wheel of the Audi A8 was a teenager no more than sixteen or seventeen, windows down, music blasting, more interested in paying attention to the screen of her cell phone than looking ahead.

"I'm gonna mess it up." When Tony didn't reply, Aris turned to face him. "Luke. He's..." She looked away, searching for words. "I think Luke wants from me what Celeste wanted from you. What she has now with you." Sighing heavily, she faced the street again. "And I'm going to mess it all up."

Tony paused so long that Aris thought she'd pushed the limits of their fragile father-daughter relationship.

"Loving your mother was never easy, honey bun. And though it was difficult at times...*most* times... loving her was the most amazing experience I've had in my life. When it was good, it was incredible. You're the living result of the best of us. But when it was bad, it was..." Tony paused again, swimming in memories. "What I do know is...Lydia Collier? She was always worth it. Always."

Aris sat frozen as she listened to her father share things his relationship with her mother that she had never known.

It was bizzare.

Because Tony didn't share. Ever.

But on this day, on this porch, after the evening sun made its descent...her father let her in.

She learned that for Tony, being a single father had been his biggest fear. Especially after losing the love of his life. He'd been angry, resentful. Faithless. He never quite recovered from the swift left hook from fate's cruel hand, and Aris was left to bear the brunt of her father's listlessness that he could never fully escape.

"I missed her too," Aris said, twisting her hands. "I didn't really know her like you did...but, inside...I missed her too."

"I know," Tony replied, sadly. "And I'm sorry that I didn't know how to fix it for you. To fix us. I was the adult in this, but I was lost for a long time…I just hope you know that I've always loved you, Aris. Even if I didn't always show you that."

"I knew, Dad," Aris whispered. "I know."

Running a hand down his face, Tony straightened his back and did what he did best—changed the subject. "Luke is a good man, honey bun. I believe that you two have genuine love for each other, and I'm happy to see that because I want you to know true happiness."

"You really think so?" Aris asked, surprised by how desperate she sounded for her father's opinion and approval of Luke.

Tony nodded curtly in lieu of a verbal response, conjuring vivid memories of the no-nonsense man who raised her. When he faced her, the look in his eyes was both serious and sincere. "Love is not about rainbows, puppies and hugs. It's about two people loving and connecting and working together each and every day of their lives and remembering that, even when they screw things up during the day, they can still screw that night and wake up to try again the next day."

"Oh…my…did Tony Collier just give a speech on…" Aris widened her eyes, and she gasped in dramatic effect. "*L-O-V-E?*"

Appearing ill at ease for half of a nanosecond, Tony cleared his throat and shook off his discomfort at her acknowledgment before shielding himself with his characteristic sarcasm. "Sheeeiiittt… it's the best one you ever gonna hear too. Believe that."

"The best one, indeed." Aris grinned at him, feeling light. "Wow, look at us. We're *bonding*." She started wiggling in celebration. "Our baes will be sooo proud."

"Our what?" His brows wrinkled. "Baes?"

"Never mind," Aris replied, laughing.

"Oh, you mean Celeste and Luke?" Shrugging, Tony relaxed his posture and playfully nudged his left shoulder against Aris's right one. "Yeah, those two are something special...so let's promise not to mess up this real, little family we finally got going now. For them or for the two of us, okay?"

Aris grinned and nudged him back. "Okay."

Aris pressed the button for her favorite radio station and sang every song, including the jingles during commercial breaks. Luke enjoyed it, knowing that Aris only sang when she was in a great state of mind, which wasn't a common occurrence. In the course of a day, she often bounced around the mood spectrum so, whenever she resembled anything close to a happy place, Luke embraced it.

"Hey," he asked when the music ended and another round of commercials began. "You need to run by your apartment and grab clothes for the week?"

"You want me to stay...the whole week?"

"I want you to stay period."

Aris blinked and looked away. "I'll just wash what I have on hand and go home Tuesday."

"You know you don't have to, right?"

"Aww," Aris said, picking up his hand and kissing it. "You're gonna wash my clothes for me?"

She batted her eyelashes and puckered her lips for a kiss. She was so cute that he had to lean over for a quick peck before confirming that he would absolutely not be washing her clothes tonight.

Aris twisted her lips and turned her attention to the radio dial on the dash to change the station. "Then give me my kiss back."

"Too late." He pressed a button on the steering wheel to lower the volume. "So baby…what do you think about staying with me? Permanently?"

She jerked her head to look at him, her eyes wide. "You want me to move in with you? Seriously?"

"You're practically living with me now, taking over just about every room."

"That's my point," she said quickly. "I make messes. Huge ones. And I'm already pretty lacking in the domestic department and cooking is not my thing. And I—" She cut herself off and shook her head in confusion before looking at him again. "You really want me to move in with you."

"I really want you." Lifting her hand, Luke kissed the back of it and smiled. "To move in with me."

Her eyes shifted to the dark road ahead.

"It's cool if you need some time to think about—"

"No," she said abruptly. "I mean, no I don't need to think. If I think too much, I—" She took a deep breath and stared at him until he turned his head and met her gaze. "Yes. I'll move in with you."

Luke's smile widened as he kissed the back of her hand again and lowered it to Aris's lap. "Now that I have your consent, the next order of business is to get a new place. We'll need more space."

"What?" She narrowed her eyes. "No, we don't. I like your apartment. Plus, it's close to my job."

"We can still stay in the area, but I was thinking about renting something bigger. Maybe a house."

"In Dunwoody?" Biting her lip, she turned away again. "I, umm...I can't afford to rent a house. The rent I pay now is pretty steep, so I wouldn't be able to contribute more than that—"

"Baby?"

"Yeah?"

"I got this. Okay?"

She shifted uncomfortably in her seat. "Okay."

"Now that you're cool with renting a house, we'll need to—"

Aris pulled her left hand from his grasp and joined it with her right one, twisting them in her lap.

"Talk to me."

She kept her eyes on the road for several minutes before she finally spoke. "It just feels like you're railroading me. I mean, I know you're not. I want to move in with you. But actually doing it? We'd have to search for a place and pack and..." She sighed. "It just feels so...so fast."

"You're right. I've been turning this over in my mind for a while, so I get that it must feel like I'm springing this on you out of nowhere. You need more time. I understand that."

"Thank you."

"In the meantime, I'll go ahead and schedule movers. Your lease is up in about two months, right? I'll handle that. As far as your furniture, we can put it in storage until we move into the house. The rest of it—clothes and all that—you can start bringing it over to my apartment this week."

Luke looked over and chuckled at Aris's warning glare. He pressed the button on the steering wheel to increase the volume of the music and reached over to grab Aris's left hand again, threading their fingers as she sat quietly and he drove the rest of the way home.

~ *4* ~

Waving to Nate and Troy, Aris shifted her car in reverse and pulled away. She drove to the parkway before pressing the volume button on her steering wheel, allowing music to surround her, the lyrics of the love song immediately evoking thoughts of Luke. At the red light, she pulled a light pink tube from her bag and flipped the visor where she peeped her starry-eyed reflection.

"Really, Aris?" she chastised herself after applying the gloss, not bothering to wipe the cheerful smile off her face. "You're *that* chick now?"

The light turned green.

Aris's foot pressed the gas pedal and she cruised past the other cars on the road, realizing that she didn't really mind being that chick.

Being Luke's chick.

Sure, it had taken her a while to get used to the idea

of taking their relationship to the next level, but Luke was right. Living together made sense. Especially since Aris had been spending every weekend and some week nights at his place for months now. At this point, the natural next step would be to merge finances and cohabitate so who was she to fight the progression?

Luke did most of the work in hunting for a house to rent, scouting neighborhoods and crunching numbers. Aris had a sneaky suspicion that Luke preferred to actually buy a house instead of renting one, but he'd kept to his promise not to move any faster than they already were. It was one thing to rent a house and something totally different to own one together...at least in Aris's mind, which had been challenged by endless rounds of *what ifs* for weeks. She refused to let those doubts consume her; entertaining them would bring additional stress she didn't need. Instead, she chose to focus on appreciating the reality that he wanted her in his life in a major way.

Aris was his and Luke was hers.

And she liked it. A lot.

It was a new feeling for her. Never once had she ever cared to be formally claimed in such a significant way. The thought of ever having to live with any of her exes always brought on an intense gag reflex because being locked down was never easy for her to swallow.

But all that changed with Luke.

Initially, yes...there were several meltdown moments but now Aris felt pretty proud of the rapid evolution of their relationship.

Live-in boyfriend and girlfriend.

Shacker-uppers. Official "we" people.

Despite the urge to flee, it made Aris smile.

Still, she kept that news to herself. Kim and Deena, who were Aris's only girlfriends, had ultimately figured it out a short while later. Their gushing support prompted Aris to cautiously confess to Tony and Celeste days later, both of whom were surprisingly pleased by the news.

Luke, on the other hand, had shared it freely with everyone he knew. He seemed pleased to refer to Aris as his lady, especially around family and close friends. It was completely overwhelming, like everything else that had happened since they transitioned to complete togetherness, but Aris had to admit how wonderful it felt to be embraced in love and acceptance by each and every person related to him by blood, affinity and friendship.

When Luke first told his family, they were at his mother's house for one of their infamous family gatherings. Aris met them a few times before but remained on edge the entire time, knowing that Luke's ex, the inimitable Jessica Knox, had once been the crown jewel of Luke's life, a woman so unfuckwitable and flawless that Aris was sure to be perceived as a sad, sorry substitute.

She couldn't have been more wrong.

The family was thrilled and jokingly hinted at them hosting the next holiday gathering at their new house. Being the recipient of such a display of unconditional love had affected Aris so much that she retreated to the furthest corner of the massive backyard to process her feelings, the area of Luke's childhood home that was quickly becoming her favorite spot while visiting. She sat quietly for several minutes, gazing up at the sky, consumed by her thoughts, when her mother-in-law casually approached and joined her without saying one word. If it had been anyone else, Aris would have thought it was a creepy move or one to intimidate her, but not Luke's mom. Sarah Donovan was genuine and didn't play games, a woman with a heart of gold. Approaching Aris's space in silence had not been a power move at all, but a deliberate act to show that she respected Aris's need for comfortable distance yet also remembered her desire to still feel connected.

She thought back to the first time Luke called her Moody in front of his mother, and all Sarah did was smile and wink at her.

The woman was beyond astute.

She faced Sarah now, who smiled and winked again.

Aris spoke first.

"You're all so close, and I was just thinking that I'm not sure I know how to do this," she said humbly. "To be a part of your family."

"There's plenty of time to figure that out, sweetie. Until then, just relax. You'll know when you know."

And that was all Aris and Sarah said to each as they shared a pitcher of lemonade in silence for the next thirty minutes. Sarah had brought a carafe and two cups before she propped her feet up on the ottoman and began to read a book, keeping Aris company but not bothering her in any way at all until she felt comfortable enough to share her feelings.

It was the day that Aris had officially fallen in love with Luke's mother.

Aris's heart tightened because her relationship with

her own father wasn't nearly as effortless though she wanted it to be. A little bit of joy slipped through her angst and she smiled to herself, recalling the first, real heart-to-heart that she recently had with Tony about Luke and Celeste.

Aris could definitely get used to this family thing.

Checking the side mirror, she exited the highway. On impulse, she grabbed her phone from the cupholder and dialed Luke's number. He answered right away.

"I need you."

Those three words made her heart skip a beat and the sound of his voice extended her smile. It was stupid how much he affected her, how much she had grown accustomed to knowing he was always there, whenever she needed him. It was the most peaceful feeling she'd ever had in her life.

"Hello to you, too, Mr. Donovan."

"Are you home yet?"

"I'm on the way right now," she replied. "You?"

"Down the street, 'bout to pull up."

"Well then you still have a few seconds to explain exactly how you're needing me right now."

Luke obliged, expressing to Aris in explicit detail everything she already expected to hear sans a handful of unexpected variances since the last time he shared how much he "needed" her.

"All that, huh?" She laughed. "Freak."

"All day. Now hurry your pretty ass up. I can show you better than I can tell you."

Ending the call, Aris continued to cruise along, purposefully disobeying Luke's request to rush home because that's just the way she was wired. Luke was sure to take notice of her playful insolence and would be waiting impatiently for her at the door, ready to respond to her sass with some brass of his own.

Her body tingled at the thought as she drove to his apartment. Aris was ready to race inside to get her fix once she cut the ignition, but her phone sounded off with Troy's name appearing on its screen.

"Hey," she answered. "What's up?"

"Baby doll, I need your brilliance," Troy said without greeting. "I'm home. Come through."

"Well you're gonna have to get my brilliance over the phone in five minutes tops 'cause I'm home too."

"Shit," he mumbled.

Aris could picture him frowning and she laughed. Troy was always so damn extra when things didn't go his way.

"Can you come back out later?" he finally asked.

"Nah."

"Oh right...you all on that shack-up shit now," he replied sarcastically. "Guess I'll just handle this mock-up all by myself then..."

"Hol'up," Aris said, tuning back in just as she entered the apartment and crossed the foyer to peck Luke on the lips. Stepping back, she held up her index finger and continued toward the master bedroom. "What mock up?"

Aris listened as Troy updated her on a new contract he landed earlier in the day that required more than his two hands to complete. Luke joined her in the bedroom, watching as she continued bantering with Troy about how his eyes were always bigger than his talent. Aris shook her head as she paused to hear whatever else Troy had to say and Luke's eyes narrowed when she was overtaken by a fit of giggles. This went on another few minutes before Aris finally noticed Luke casually leaning against his dresser with his arms crossed, expressionless.

"Whatever, dude. Yeah. Cool. Yeeesss, I just said I'll help you...just not tonight. I'm busy right now." Aris glanced at Luke. "You got me tomorrow afternoon, all right? Yeah. Later."

Still chuckling, Aris hung up the phone and smiled brightly, still considering the new project Troy lucked up on. She had been dying to do that type of work and was thrilled that Troy knew better than to take it on without involving her, but the look on Luke's face caused her to dial back her glee.

"Troy," Aris explained with a smirk. "He's got a new project, and I'm gonna help him with it."

"He's got you tomorrow," Luke replied as he observed her. "Yeah. I caught that."

Aris blinked, uncertain if Luke meant anything by his comment or if he was simply confirming what he'd heard her say. Before she could think too much about it, her gaze dropped to his open, collared shirt and the black tank underneath hugging his body. When her eyes lifted back up to his face, she grinned wickedly.

"And you, Mr. Donovan," she began as she strutted towards him. "Will have me all evening, all night and all morning."

Luke didn't move an inch and watched Aris come closer, his face still impassive but his eyes giving her the green light to proceed. When her lips touched his, Luke's hands gripped her waist and what she thought would be a teasing peck transformed into a deep, rhythmic kiss. For the next minute, he made love to her mouth the way she was ready to make love to him. Moaning, Aris nipped his bottom lip and eased back in an attempt to grab his dick and move things along, but Luke gripped her tighter as he lowered his head and stole her breath for the next few minutes before leading her to the bed. Her body trembled in response, the passion between them beginning to feel more like a power struggle.

Luke needed Aris to cave to him...and she did.

They lay tangled in the sheets afterwards, clothing strewn all over the floor in their haste. Aris snuggled closer to Luke, enjoying the pressure of his hand caressing the curve of her ass.

"I'm gonna miss the hell out of you, baby."

"I know," she replied before dropping a light kiss on his chest. "I hate when you travel without me."

"I don't have to travel without you. You know that."

Aris sighed, regretting that she unwittingly triggered the ongoing debate between them. As much as she enjoyed tagging along on Luke's business trips when time permitted, Aris no longer had the flexibility. The schedule for her main gig was notably unpredictable, not to mention the chaos of taking on random projects and contracts like the ones that Troy just landed.

"I do," she confirmed. "I appreciate it, too."

Silence covered them as minutes ticked by.

"I can fly you up Friday afternoon," Luke offered. "Make it a weekend."

The suggestion sounded perfect, but she needed that time to make some headway with Troy. "I got a lot on my plate so just come home Friday. We already planned to draw up some sketches on Saturday for this set we got tapped for." She snuggled against him and kissed his chest. "Man, it's gonna be so dope." When Luke didn't respond, Aris looked up. "Wanna come with me? It'll only be for a few hours. Then, we can catch that Marvel movie or something after that before we go home so I can finish working."

"You and Troy... again."

Aris didn't respond.

"Nate too?"

"Nate has a girl now and officially lost his mind, so he's been dialing back on the man hours lately." When Luke grunted, Aris stared at him with a knowing expression. "Yeah, we're giving him a pass 'cause I bailed on them the same way when I spent that week with you in Vegas." She laughed and kissed him gingerly. "I totally get it."

"Do you?"

Aris blinked at the irritation lacing Luke's voice. "Of course. That's why I'm covering for Nate like he did for me. It's my turn to step up and, at some point, Troy will get caught up with some chick and fall off too...then me and Nate will take up the slack."

"Troy falling off?" Luke pushed out a humorless laugh. "Yeah. Not happening."

Aris sat up. There was no mistaking what was beneath Luke's sarcasm. She pinned him with a wide-eyed gaze and Luke stared back at her pointedly as if she was missing the obvious. They squared off for several seconds until her eyes lit up in amusement. "Oh wait...you think Troy is gay or something?" Her giggles tumbled out before turning into a full laugh. "I can see how you might come up with that, but nah baby…Troy is not gay. A bit of a weirdo, yes, but that's just him though. Seriously, he's completely straight."

"Glad to know you're actually aware of that fact."

There it was again.

Aris frowned at Luke's tone.

"What are you trying to say?"

"That you're acting like this dude is like Deena or some shit. He's not your girlfriend, baby…he's still a man." Luke waited for her to respond, but Aris looked away. "You hearing me?"

Taking a deep breath, Aris relaxed her face as best she could and looked at him. "I'm hearing that you're being a little extra right now. You haven't even met Troy and Nate for that matter."

"I'm being *your man* right now, and I need to know that you hear me when I tell you these things not because I'm trying to micromanage your situations but because I love you and I will protect us at all costs."

"Protect us? From what? Weird-ass Troy?" She shook her head in earnest to counter his argument. "Baby, trust me. You are way off base."

Her amusement returned, followed by more laughter, but Aris quieted as soon as she saw Luke's jaw clench. Refusing to entertain such nonsense, Aris sighed dramatically while pulling the bedsheet from her body. It was time to take a page out of Luke's book.

She could show him better than she could tell him.

"Baby," Aris began, staring into his eyes. "I hear you. But I also need you to hear me. I give zero fucks about Troy like that. He's a friend and we work together."

She ran a finger down the bridge of his nose. "He's not you." She kissed his lips. "He's never been you." She slowly trailed her lips down his chest. "And he will never be you."

Before Luke could protest, Aris dropped her head and took him into her mouth.

"*Shit*...baby..."

Looking up, Aris paused her assault and caught his eyes. "I love you. You're it for me. Always and forever, Lucas James Donovan. Got it?"

All Luke could do was nod and moan his response.

Satisfied, Aris smiled and went back to work.

~ 5 ~

"The fuck?"

Luke scowled as he read the latest text message from Aris. Pissed, he turned his phone face down on the table, ignored Devin's questioning stare and trained his gaze on the television hanging above the bar.

Seconds later, Jessica arrived with Aubrey by her side who immediately sat next to Devin. After Jessica gave Luke and Devin quick hugs, Luke stood to allow her the inside seat on his side of the booth.

Old college friends reunited once again.

In town on business, Jessica suggested they catch up with Aubrey who had been Portland home for the past two years. The ladies immediately engaged Devin in animated conversation with lots of jokes and laughter while Luke directed his attention to his phone.

As Luke tapped out another text message to Aris, Aubrey forced him to join the conversation. "Stop being rude, Luke. I haven't seen you in forever... tell me something good."

Luke raised his head, offering an apologetic nod before dropping his gaze to finish his text message. "Life's good. Grinding with D to get this business off the ground. The A has been good to us, so I'm looking to stick around. Been on the hunt for a house the last few weeks—"

"Oh my God!" Aubrey squealed, clapping her hands. "Jess, why didn't you tell me y'all were buying a spot in Atlanta? No wonder y'all shady asses hit me up out of nowhere to come hang...I'm guessing it's about that time to jump that broom!" When Luke tried to interrupt, Aubrey raised her hand with a knowing smile. "So our roles are pretty obvious—Bride, Groom, Best Man and, ahem...moi, the Forever Fabulous Maid of Honor...but when the hell is the wedding?" The table got deadly quiet as Aubrey glared pointedly at Jessica's bare left hand. "And what's up with the ring? You still searching for the perfect rock or something?"

While Devin and Luke sat calmly with blank expressions, Jessica took it upon herself to swiftly and graciously explain that yes, Luke was permanently living in Atlanta now and yes, he was looking for a house...but with someone else.

Aubrey almost spit out her drink, choking as Devin pulled the glass from her hand and sat it on the table. Waving off Luke and Jessica's concern at her coughing fit, Aubrey finally caught her breath and cast a crazed expression at Devin. "What the hell...are they high?"

"Nah," Devin replied easily, grinning as he settled back against the booth.

After a few seconds, Aubrey fell back against the booth with a dazed expression on her face as she looked from Luke to Jessica and back again. "This can't be life…"

"Girl, relax," Jessica finally said, shaking her head in amusement. "Honestly, I'm surprised the news hadn't gotten around to you yet. Shit, felt like the world blew my phone up when we called it quits. How long ago has it been now, Luke…a little over a year?"

Luke tapped the screen of his phone a few more times before putting it away and looking up to glance at Jessica. "Yeah. About that long."

"Wow." Baffled, Aubrey shook her head. "And you're here now. Together? You're…*friends*?"

"As opposed to what?" Jessica asked curiously before taking a dainty sip of her margarita.

"I just…I'm sorry. I…this is just blowing my mind right now, but if you're happy, then I'm happy." She turned to Dez in a conspiratorial whisper. "They *are* happy…right?"

"Very happy," Luke and Jessica said in unison as they clinked their glasses while Devin laughed heartily at Aubrey's reaction.

"Damn, this is the fucking twilight zone for real," Aubrey replied before taking a long sip from her own glass. "But hey…it is what it is. Luke, congrats to you and your new lady who, I would imagine, must be beyond amazing to have you house-hunting already."

Luke finally smiled. "She is. Her name is Aris."

"Cool name," Aubrey replied, taking another sip. "So what does she do?"

Luke laughed as Aubrey, Jessica and Devin stared at

him, wondering if they'd missed the punch line.

"Nah, it's nothing." Luke shook his head, still chuckling. "Aris hates when people ask that question. Anyway, she's a make-up artist. TV, film, all that."

"Wasn't she on a reality show too?" Jessica asked. Luke nodded, and she turned bright eyes to Aubrey. "I think they're showing reruns of the last season. Aris's work is incredible; you should check it out. I was impressed after these two clowns got me hooked. It's a really good show."

"Wooow." Aubrey looked between Luke and Jessica again, shaking her head in disbelief. "You have no idea how much I appreciate seeing this."

"Seeing what?" Jessica asked.

"True friendship, no matter what," Aubrey replied, admiration in her eyes. "It's a beautiful thing." She raised her glass as Luke, Jessica and Devin joined her.

"To true friendship," Aubrey toasted. "Cheers!"

Don't be like that...I'll call you as soon as I get home.

That was the last message Luke received from Aris.

A text she sent him over two hours ago.

And he was still waiting for her to call.

As a result, Luke had returned to the foul mood he was in before Jessica and Aubrey had arrived to join him and Devin for dinner. He'd been grateful for the good food and even better conversation after the ladies arrived, a welcome distraction after having learned from Aris that Troy not only got Aris's afternoon but the entire evening and, now, half the night as well.

And she still hadn't called him…

Grabbing his beer, Luke finished it off and ordered another. After dinner, the friends split up again with Jessica and Aubrey on their way to a new music lounge while Devin and Luke searched for a local sports bar to catch a game. They had been there for the past hour, Luke in his feelings while Devin entertained a woman sitting next to him in hopes of taking her back to his hotel room for the night.

While Troy entertained Aris…

Luke cursed himself and leaned back from the bar, annoyed with how ridiculously territorial he was feeling at that moment. He knew better than to work himself up like this but, despite his best efforts, Luke could not shake his aggravation at Troy's opportunistic ass being so available to Aris whenever Luke wasn't.

Luke hadn't even met the dude and he despised him.

The bartender delivered a fresh beer, and Luke grabbed it and consumed almost half the bottle in one, long gulp.

He needed to get his shit together.

This wasn't the first time Aris had him in a tailspin. Luke could easily recall the initial stages of their friendship and how, even then, she drove him crazy. During that time, he'd still been involved with Jessica and fought his attraction to Aris with everything in him, but nothing worked. There was just something about her that kept him hooked.

Luke had to have her.

And Troy was likely hooked as well. Aris had that effect; it was effortless. The poor bastard was probably experiencing the same obsessive interest and reckless desire, especially with all the extra time Troy had been spending with her while he was out of town.

Cursing again, Luke finished his beer.

It never failed to unnerve him how many dudes tried him to get next to Aris. It was damn near comical. Not that he hadn't experienced something similar before with Jessica, because he had...he just never had to worry given her ability to shut shit down in and out of his presence. With Jessica, he'd been completely at ease. Not to mention that she also had a cagey, elusive quality about her, the type of woman a man would only ever fantasize about but never attempt to touch.

Aris, on the other hand, was the polar opposite.

Hers was a different type of beauty, the enticing and approachable kind that almost begged a man to engage and bypass a touch for a taste. Aris had a way of making everyone around her feel special, similar to how she had charmed him senseless when they first met. Luke had no idea how to corral that and the fact that he actually had to was beyond frustrating. Every day, he felt pressed to somehow control it—control her—which put a further strain on their budding relationship. It felt like the equivalent of trying to trap a butterfly in a jar, but Luke quickly learned how futile that was. That you can't trap a butterfly without hurting it...and the last thing he ever wanted to do was hurt Aris.

A controlling man, Luke was not. He never had been. That was something he frowned upon—men who were so insecure that they went to great lengths to keep their women under lock and key.

Luke was not that guy.

But Troy was definitely an issue.

One he refused to allow to become a problem.

Luke simply needed Aris to recognize that and always be ready to shut it down, from Troy to any other man who refused to fall back because he wouldn't always be around to do it...and he shouldn't have to be.

"I would ask if you wanna talk about it," Devin said, interrupting Luke's thoughts. "But I just remembered I currently and fully reject the idea of living under the same roof as any woman so shit, man...I got nothing."

Luke chuckled and took another sip of his beer. "Just keep the drinks comin', man...that's all I need."

~ 6 ~

SEPTEMBER

Adjusting the silk scarf on her head, Aris stared at her reflection in the mirror before bending to splash water on her face. She cracked one eye open, reached over to pump a few squirts of foaming facial cleanser into her wet hands and applied it to her face. Once she was done, she rinsed with water several times and turned off the faucet. Her hand found the washcloth on the counter and patted her face dry before pumping a few squirts of moisturizer to massage into her face. Running her tongue over her teeth, she turned the faucet back on and grabbed her toothbrush to apply a minty fresh paste to rid the taste of wine from her mouth. A swig of mouthwash later and she was finally ready for bed.

Aris padded from the bathroom into the bedroom and slipped between the cool sheets. The television was on but muted. Not so much for entertainment as it was to help her feel less alone with Luke across the country on another business trip. Despite the scientific "lights out for quality sleep" argument, Aris found the people inside her television to be pretty soothing companions during the night.

Laying her head on the pillow, she closed her eyes and tried to block out the racing thoughts in her head. Her plan had been to get in bed at a decent hour and give her body the rest it truly needed so she could wake with the understanding of what eight solid hours sleep really felt like.

She was on her way to achieving that said plan...

But a bump in the night forced her eyes to open.

Aris immediately looked at the security system keypad on the wall. The red light signaled that nothing had ventured inside, but it didn't guarantee that it would stay that way. She listened carefully, the sound of her beating heart loud in her eyes, the people in the television carrying on with their latest crime scene investigation, causing her to wonder if she might soon play the starring role in a real-life version of the show.

Aris heard another loud noise, not quite a bump but something strange, something much louder, like an animal was nearby, rummaging around.

Or a human.

Aris heard the harsh, ragged breaths, the burst of air rushing in and out of her flared nostrils, felt the tremors passing through her body. It seemed to take all of her strength just to breathe. She was paralyzed.

Another noise.

More than a bump but less than a thump. An

unidentifiable noise now right outside her window one story below.

She focused on the main source of light in the room.

The people in the television were worthless when it really mattered.

They had to go.

Aris snatched the remote from the bed and quickly pressed the OFF button. In an instant, she was bathed in darkness and an even greater silence.

She waited. Listened.

Unable to move, her brain in temporary limbo, she warred with herself. Internally debating the age-old fight or flight response while subconsciously choosing the third option – to freeze.

Minutes passed.

Breathing calmed.

Brain was back in the game.

Aris reached blindly for the cordless phone on her nightstand and pressed TALK. The last number appeared on the screen. She pressed TALK again. Waited for the spaced tones to give way to a voice.

"Hey, Moody."

She found her own voice. "Luke."

There was activity in his background, what sounded like silverware connecting with plates and people connecting with other people.

"Hold on, baby…I can barely hear you."

Her eyes shifted through the darkness toward the glare of red digital numbers a few feet away on Luke's side of the bed. She had forgotten about the time difference. Though she was thirteen minutes into a new day, he was still enjoying the last few hours of the old one.

Soon, the background noise was gone. It was as quiet as it was on her end of the phone.

"All right...had to step away. We're still at this dinner. The service is slow as hell." He sounded calm but tired. "You okay? I'm guessing the implementation of your sleep-before-ten plan isn't going so well?"

"I heard something. Outside the house. It woke me up. But..." She paused and took a deep breath, hoping to ease the trill in her voice. "I think it's fine now. Whatever it was, I think it's gone."

She listened as Luke launched into interrogation mode. By the end of their tense exchange, she realized her mistakes. He pointed them out, an increasing level of stress lacing each word of his measured speech. When he was done, she hung up. Dialed 911. Took a few moments to explain what little she had heard to the dispatcher, asked that they send the police. She hung up and dialed Luke again. He answered and it was still quiet in his background. Then she heard him thank someone. Heard that someone thank him and wish him a good night.

He had left the dinner.

She hadn't meant for him to do that. She only wanted to hear his voice, to feel better.

She told him exactly that.

"It's fine, baby," Luke assured her. "Fuck that dinner. It was almost over anyway. You're more important."

That made her smile.

"Are the police on their way?"

"Yes."

"Good. Keep me on the phone, even when the officer

gets there. Don't hang up."

"Okay."

They chatted until the squad car arrived. Twenty minutes of casual conversation about Luke's client adventures, some of which she understood but most of it she didn't. Luke did all of the talking, on purpose perhaps and Aris was grateful...the sound of his voice soothing her frayed nerves.

The doorbell rang.

"They're here," she announced, climbing out of bed.

"That was quick. Put me on speaker phone before you answer the door."

She did as instructed. After answering the door, the three of them—Aris, Luke's voice and the police officer—asked and answered a series of questions before the officer instructed Aris to close and lock the door while he and his partner did a perimeter check of the house. Several minutes later, there was a knock at the door and both officers were standing there. Luke's voice blared through the speaker of Aris's phone, requesting the officers to search the interior anyway despite there not being any visible signs of forced entry or damage from the outside of the house. The officers complied and Aris let them inside, closing and locking the door behind them. They searched every square inch of the house and returned to the foyer where Aris remained. Satisfied, Luke's voice said thank you and Aris said goodbye to the officers. Both men nodded, reminding her to arm the security system and to call again should she experience further concerns.

She watched the tail lights of the squad car disappear down the street before turning off the lights and climbing the stairs. Once inside the bedroom, she armed the security system and climbed into bed, leaving Luke on speaker because it felt more like he was in the room with her.

Luke's voice was a million times better than the muted companionship of the people in her television.

"Are you tired?"

"Yeah," he replied. "But I'll get to bed soon enough. I want to make sure you're asleep first."

Aris smiled at the picture of him on her cell phone screen. His eyes were staring right at her. She missed him. "I am not falling asleep on this phone."

"Sure you're not."

She stared up at the ceiling fan, the glow from her cell phone casting a shadow along the walls. "I guess I'm still not used to this house."

"That's understandable. It's only been two weeks." He paused. "You have no idea how much I wish I was there with you right now."

"Me too."

Another pause. "Other than this midnight scare, how was the rest of your day?"

She replayed each mundane marker of her day, in color detail that amused him and produced a laugh here and there. After about an hour, she could tell that he was struggling to stay awake. He had been up since 4AM, going nonstop all day. She checked the clock again. It was nearing midnight where he was. He still had to be up in another five hours to do everything he had done yesterday all over again.

"Luke...go to sleep."

"Nah, I'm good."

"Sure you are."

He pushed out a weak laugh before it turned into a yawn. "Are you even the least bit tired?"

"Nope."

"Ahh baby...I'm sorry. It's been a really long day."

"I know. You gotta get some rest. I'll be fine."

"I believe that." He groaned. Sounded like he was stretching. "Just know that I'm here, baby. If anything else happens, call the police and then call me...okay?"

"Sir, yes sir."

Another weak laugh. Another yawn.

An extended exchange of love yous and miss yous.

Then, she was alone again.

Aris woke with a start.

Her breathing was ragged again, her heart almost beating out of her chest.

It took a moment for her to register that someone wasn't actually inside the house. Her nightmare had felt so real that she debated calling the police again. But what would she tell them? That she *dreamed* someone had broken in and was trying to kill her?

She grabbed the phone and pressed TALK. Luke's number appeared on screen but she paused. Fell back against the pillows holding the phone to her chest. As much as she wanted to hear his voice, she didn't want to wake him. He would worry, then he wouldn't sleep and then he'd be a wreck all day because of her.

All because she was spooked.

Exhaling a weary breath, she checked the clock again. Though it felt like she'd been asleep awhile, only an hour had passed. She lay in the dark for twenty minutes, the phone pressed to her chest.

She really was spooked.

So she called Kim.

After she got cursed out for waking up her friend, Kim chatted with her for about thirty minutes before she too succumbed to sleep.

Then, Aris was alone again.

Still spooked.

Turning over onto her side, she thought about doing what Kim had suggested, but getting a hotel room this late and wasting the money sounded ridiculous. Spooked or not, that was definitely not happening.

So, she got over it.

At least she tried to.

But a whole ten minutes passed and she was still on edge despite hanging with the people in her television. It surprised her, how unsettled she felt. Once upon a time, she delighted in living alone and sleeping alone. But then her apartments had always been fairly small, with people above and below her in some cases, so she was never really alone. Sure, she and Luke had neighbors but there was a bit of distance between the houses, divided by trees. If someone were to break in, her neighbors may not hear her until it was too late…

"Stop it," Aris mumbled to herself.

But she was still spooked.

After considerable thought and a brief hesitation, she swapped the cordless house phone for her cell phone and dialed a familiar number. Waited for the spaced tones to give way to another voice.

"Yo," Troy said groggily when he answered. "You better be on the side of the road or some shit…"

"Umm, no." Aris released a long, shaky breath, still uncertain about her next words but she said them anyway. "Can I crash there for the rest of the night?"

"Can you…wait, what?"

She heard rustling in his background.

"You want to crash here? What's going on, baby doll…did something happen? Where are you? Are you all right?"

"I'm home and I'm fine. Well, not really. I'm just a little freaked out 'cause it sounded like someone was trying to break in here earlier and Luke's away on business and I'm having nightmares and trippin' and…" Noticing her rambling, she frowned. "Can I come over or not? You got company?"

"Ain't nobody here," he said, irritation in his voice. "Do you need me to come get you? I'm not feelin' you being on the road this late."

"I can make it. I'm on my way." She hopped out of bed. "I'll be there in thirty."

"All right. Let yourself in."

"Cool." She paused. "And Troy?"

"Yeah?"

"Thank you."

"No problem. I always got you, baby doll."

She hung up and began tossing a few items in a duffle bag. Fifteen minutes later, she was backing out of the garage. On the road, her mind got the best of her and she began questioning her decision but quickly got over it. Going to Troy's was much easier than trying to get a hotel room this time of night. And it wasn't like she had anywhere else to go. Nate was the only other friend she had in town besides Kyle and both of them were probably laid up with their women. She didn't want to impose. Troy was a crap shoot; if he had someone in his bed too, she would've gotten through the rest of the night as best she could.

Luckily, she didn't have to.

Because Troy was as alone as she was.

~ 7 ~

Aris let herself into Troy's apartment for the second time in twelve hours.

She removed the key from the lock and dropped it into her bag. It was the same key Troy had given her a few weeks ago because it was easier than his lazy ass having to open the door for her whenever she got the urge to stop by. Aris often teased him that she'd better not walk in one day to see the back of his ass between some random THOT's thighs. Troy laughed in response, saying he didn't know she cared so much to which she quickly dismissed with a flip of her hand, explaining that there was just some shit she never, *ever* ever, wanted to know about him.

Aris had just returned from getting a sketch pad from her car. Not wanting to be irresponsible, she decided to lock the front door on her way out, just in case there was someone lurking somewhere nearby, waiting to take advantage of her carelessness and blanket trust in humanity. Sure, she was only making a quick trip to the parking lot but anything could happen...which was why she was still camped out at Troy's and had not returned home yet.

Apparently, the spook hadn't worn off.

It multiplied and morphed into paranoia.

The high noon sun beamed through the windows. So many windows. Aris decided long ago that this was a great apartment, perfect in fact. Definitely a place she would have chosen for herself if she was still solo and the recipient of a bigger paycheck. But since she was neither of those things, Aris was left to live vicariously through Troy...and take advantage of his generosity and willingness to allow her free reign of his place as long as she called first.

After making a smoothie, Aris left the kitchen and collapsed onto the sofa in the living room.

Headphones in. Time to get back to work.

Troy walked through the front door about twenty minutes later, but she was so focused that she didn't hear him enter. One minute Aris was in a zone, flowing...the next, she heard his deep baritone break through and shatter her awesome bubble.

She jumped and abruptly turned her head toward his voice, attempting to put distance between Troy's mouth and her ear but inadvertently increasing the weirdness now that her mouth was wide open and just an inch or two from his smirking lips.

Then, her body did the strangest thing.

It reacted instantly, tingling from the close call. Disturbed, Aris blamed her reaction on the surprise of it all, but when she shifted her gaze from his lips to his dark eyes, something that could only be best described as carnal passed between them. Aris frowned at the feeling, unable to look away as they held each other's gaze much longer than necessary.

Grinning at her response, Troy moved away from her. "What have I told you about zoning out like that when I'm not here...especially when you haven't set the alarm?"

"What? One of your psycho baes gonna come gouge my eyes out for being in here or something? Whatever. I knew you would be back soon." She turned her head to watch him enter the kitchen. "Aww, look at you... caring about me and stuff. If this was coming from anyone else, I'd say that was totes adorbs, but since it's you..." She narrowed her eyes and tilted her head at the serious expression she saw on his face. "You're really serious, aren't you?"

"I am," he replied, deadpan. "I wouldn't forgive myself if something happened to you...especially while you're with me. You really gotta start paying more attention to your surroundings, baby doll."

"Okay, fiiine." Aris released a long, audible breath. "I'll remember to set the alarm and be on alert when you're not here. Satisfied?"

Troy nodded, accepting her verbal agreement. "I got some food," he said after a few moments of silence. "You hungry? Oh shit...dumb question."

She ignored his thinly veiled insult. "What you got?"

He appeared again with her favorite snack in hand and she began bouncing up and down in excitement. "No. You. Didn't. Yeeesss! Man...you might be a little bit of all right with me, Troy Murphy. Thank youuu!"

After Troy put up a few items in the kitchen, he returned to the sofa and lifted Aris's feet and put them in his lap. She felt his eyes on her but didn't meet his gaze until she was at a good breaking point in her work. Turning her laptop around, she smiled brightly. "Check it out."

He nodded his head in appreciation. "On point as always. Where'd you get the idea from?"

"Just popped in my head and, once I sat down, it just came out. I'm beginning to think I do my best work over here...I might have to claim one of your bedrooms pretty soon."

Before he could respond, her phone buzzed. Swinging her feet to the floor, she glanced at the screen and answered right away.

"I miss you, Donovan."

"I miss you too," Luke replied, a smile in his voice. "How's my baby? You made it through the night?"

Aris glanced at Troy before looking away. "Yep. I'm good. All is well."

"Anything else happen that I should know about?"

She paused, shifting the phone from one ear to the other. "Umm, no. No, not really...like what? What do you mean?"

"The house...no more bumps in the night, I hope?"

She released her breath. Smiled. "Nope. I guess I was just hearing things."

"Maybe, maybe not," Luke replied. "If it happens again, I don't want you to hesitate to call the police. I need you to be and always feel safe."

"I'm safe."

"Good. Are you still at home?"

She cleared her throat, glanced at Troy again before looking down at her hands. "No. I'm at Troy's right now, working on this contract stuff."

Luke's silence was punctuated by a grunt.

"I won't be here much longer," she added. "I've got an appointment downtown at six-thirty."

"That's great, baby...for the show?"

"Actually, it's with a new client. There's a celebrity fundraiser coming up in two weeks and she wants more of a fun look...said I came highly recommended, but she wouldn't tell me who until we meet up later."

"That's...weird."

"They're all weird," she said, shrugging. "Such is celebrity life. I'm still trippin' that she actually called *me* though...it's huge. Guess who it is?"

Luke spent a minute or two playing "guess who" before she spilled the beans. "Are you shittin' me?" he asked, impressed.

Aris laughed. "My same exact words to her when she told me who she was when she called."

"Well, she obviously sees what I see in you," Luke praised. "I'm proud of you, baby. Told you it was just a matter of time before people started checkin' for you."

Aris beamed, a brilliant smile stretching across her face until she turned to see Troy staring at her, a smirk on his lips. She cleared her throat again. "Thanks, babe. I'll call you when it's over, tell you how it went and how she is. I hope she's as cool as she seems."

"Cool, do that. I've got another dinner tonight but I'm available whenever. Hold on..."

She listened as he had a brief conversation with what

sounded like two or three people. Soon, he was speaking into the phone, telling her he had to go. Told her that he was sorry that hadn't had their usual talk time because he didn't want to wake her up too early after such a restless night, that after his dinner obligation he would be all hers tonight and back in her arms tomorrow.

As he talked, Aris justified her earlier omission about the details of her night and her decision to spend the rest of it in Troy's apartment. It wasn't that big of a deal, really. Plus, she didn't want him to worry that she wasn't comfortable in the house just yet, especially with him traveling so much lately. No need to worry him unnecessarily. Besides, nothing happened. It was probably all in her head. She would return home after her client meeting and simply let it go. She was safe.

They exchanged love yous and miss yous.

One more day and Luke would be home.

Hanging up, she felt Troy's eyes on her.

"How long do I have you?" he asked, casually.

"Long enough to help me prep for this meeting I have with ole girl," she replied, tearing into her snack. "Please? I don't want to fuck this up."

"Not possible," he assured her. "You don't know how to fail."

Aris relaxed her shoulders and smiled.

"Now," Troy said. "Tell me what's on your mind."

A flood of ideas tumbled from Aris's mouth as though she couldn't share them fast enough. Earlier that morning over breakfast, she got him up to speed on the client's needs and other details of her initial conversation. Now, she needed his opinion on her pitch and overall approach as well as feedback about next steps.

Stretching out on the sofa, Aris repositioned her sock-covered feet in Troy's lap and talked nonstop as he listened and helped her research the client, develop a clear strategy and brainstorm the possibilities.

~ 8 ~

Nothing to do but wait.

In the quiet night, Aris lay awake in her bed, pretending not to study the clock on Luke's nightstand. Just as a new hour was beginning, she heard the sound of a car door slam.

Excitement welled up in her chest.

Luke was home.

It was later than expected due to a flight delay thanks to storms hovering over the west coast. Aris could only imagine how tired Luke was now, which was why she was awake and impatiently waiting for him.

The main reason?

She missed the hell out of him.

And she had every intention of showing him just how much, to do whatever possible to relax him, to make him feel her love, before he flew off again early Monday morning.

Aris tossed the covers back and hopped out of bed. Checked her reflection in the dresser mirror, primped a bit then rushed out of the bedroom and down the hall before she came to a stop, her eyes glued to the front door as it opened and closed and Luke stepped into view. "Hey baby. I missed you."

Luke paused, staring at her. No words.

It was too dark to read the expression on his face, but Aris didn't bother wasting more time gauging his mood. Without pause, she closed the distance between them and slipped into his arms.

Luke pulled her closer to him, squeezing Aris until she giggled then dropped his chin on the top of her head. "I missed you too, baby. I'm exhausted."

"I know."

Stepping back, Aris bent down to grab the handle of his suitcase and rolled it further into the house.

"What are you doing?" Luke asked, amused.

"Hurry," she commanded. "You're wasting time."

Luke caught up with Aris and removed his rolling suitcase from her grasp, picking it up and following her up the stairs and into their bedroom. He sat on the edge of the bed as she instructed then waited patiently as she removed his shoes, socks and shirt. When Aris attacked his pants, struggling to get them off, Luke asked if he could help. Frowning, she caved to his suggestion, allowing to him to assist her for that single task before she finished the rest and commanded him to chill while she turned her attention back to his suitcase to unpack. Luke did as he was told, grinning as he watched Aris flutter around the bedroom, toss his clothes into the laundry hamper and ensure that everything else was returned to its proper place.

Proud of herself, Aris moved back to the bed and grabbed Luke's hand, leading him into the bathroom toward the shower where Luke dropped his boxers and she stripped. When they stepped into the shower together, Luke's eyes lit up and Aris smacked his bare ass and grinned. "None of that, mister. I'm taking care of you right now."

Luke opened his mouth, but Aris pressed a finger to his lips to stop his protest. "I know. I miss you too, but I got this. Trust me, okay?"

He didn't respond, just watched as she proceeded to work up a lather with a bar of soap and a washcloth. She took her time caressing and cleaning every inch of them both, batting Luke's hands as he tried to shift her attention to a more sensual activity. Aris obliged him with a kiss that lingered a bit too long, one that had him switch tactics and press her body against the shower wall, his mouth and hands all over her. As much as she wanted to feel him after a week of need, she already had her mind made up about how this night was going to end. There would be plenty of time for them to make love this weekend, but right now was not the time.

Aris pressed her finger against the crease between Luke's brows when he backed away from her. That predatory look was still in his eyes, but he nodded in concession, signaling his cooperation. Smiling, Aris stepped out of the shower and wrapped a towel around her body before grabbing another to dry him. He insisted on drying her as well so she let him...until it began to feel more like caresses and fondling resulting in her smacking his bare ass once again to keep things under control.

"I can't help it," he said, pressing his mouth on her neck. "Have you seen you?"

More kisses and she almost caved again.

Almost.

Frustrated, Luke stepped back and rubbed a hand over his head before a sheepish grin appeared on his face. "Okay. Since I can't touch you right now, what can I do?"

"You...," Aris began. "Can stop talking and go sit in the chair for me. Pretty please?"

Luke laughed and shook his head as Aris batted her eyelashes. He headed toward the recliner in the corner of the room, leaving her to finish what she started. When she finally emerged from the bathroom, Luke's eyes narrowed at the towels and additional items in her hands.

"Sssshhhh," she said again before he could speak.

Several minutes later, Luke was rendered speechless as hot towels were wrapped about both of his feet. He glanced down at Aris, sitting on a small stool in front of him, arranging bottles and more towels on the carpeted floor. She looked up and smiled before tapping the side of the chair in a silent request for him to recline. He did as she asked, stretching out and relaxing even more.

Before Luke could ask what made her think of doing this, Aris quickly removed the towel from his right foot and began her massage.

"*Damn...*"

"Feels good, huh?" Aris replied with a smile in her

voice. "Yeah. Thought I'd surprise you with some new shit. Mmhmm...you're welcome."

"Thank you, baby. Your hands are amazing..."

Aris laughed to herself as Luke's eyes eventually closed, a clear sign that her plan had worked. She spent the next forty-five minutes alternating between both feet, one encased in a hot towel while the other was in her hands. Before long, Luke was knocked out.

Mission Accomplished.

After cleaning up, Aris tied up her hair and got ready for bed. Luke was still asleep, so she eased into bed and pressed her body against his, happy to have him home with her.

"Baby," he mumbled, pulling her close. "I love you."

Aris smiled and closed her eyes. "I love you, too."

After a morning run, Luke entered the house and paused at the mess in the living room floor. Aris in the middle of it, as usual.

"Yeah," he said, scratching his head. "I think you've met your freak show quota for the day."

"I just wanted to get this out of the way before I leave." She looked up at him expectantly. "Are you coming?"

He wanted to say yes but shook his head instead. As much as Luke felt a need to physically make his presence known, he thought back to the decision he made at the sports bar in Portland and again this morning during his run—to ease up and allow Aris to handle Troy and to trust that she would. "Nah. I'll catch the next one."

Her face fell and he softened, satisfied with knowing that she really had wanted him to come along. She blinked then pinned him with a suspicious stare before shrugging if off and returning to her work. "Okay."

Luke stretched and made his way down the hall. "I'm starving, Moody. Gonna take a shower and then make breakfast. Meet me in the kitchen in twenty."

He ignored her grumbling as he kept moving and entered the bedroom. The bed wasn't made up, of course, but he decided to let it go because it was Saturday. Discipline was not Aris's strong suit, but Luke tried his best not to ride her about the obvious things that were so unnecessary. Like leaving dirty dishes in the sink overnight. And using toilet paper until there was only one-point-five sheets left on the roll...then walking away without replacing it with a new one. Not to mention, his absolute favorite peeve... hanging a garbage bag on the knob of the pantry door instead of putting it *inside* the trash bin.

Not that Aris was the only culprit. Luke was certain that there were things that he did that annoyed her too. Sharing space and living together was hard work, and it was the first time that either of them had done such a thing. It was far from easy but, as much as some things unnerved him, Luke wouldn't trade what he had with Aris for anything in the world.

Intimacy.

It was an addictive, beautiful thing.

Much different from commitment but equally, if not more, important.

Luke definitely knew commitment. He'd spent a full eight, affectionate, companionable, organized years with Jessica.

Glancing around the bedroom and noticing Aris's collection of stacked, empty red plastic cups on top of one of the nightstands and a pile of her dirty laundry on the floor nearby, Luke shook his head and grinned.

This was *definitely* not that.

This was a thousand times better.

With Aris, he connected in ways he always thought to be fiction. Luke had never been so attached to any one person before, spending a series of passionate, messy, baffling, scary, exhausting, frisky, sometimes sleepless, oftentimes obsessive, always satisfying days and nights together and treasuring each and every one.

With Aris, Luke was in love.

A love that was far from easy but always worth it.

Stepping into the shower, he smiled and reflected on how equally challenging it had been for Aris to adjust to their relationship. She struggled daily with the level of closeness they'd reached, with her latest and most stubborn act of rebellion being her refusal to pee with the door open. Luke made it a point to barge in as much as he could, laughing each time she blessed him with that adorable little scowl and a middle finger, yelling for him to get out.

Luke, on the other hand, was wide open. It was nothing for him to waltz into the bathroom while she was taking a shower or getting dressed, flip the lid of the toilet, whip himself out and drain the main vein. Yet, despite his openness, Aris always made sure the door was properly closed and that Luke never heard nary a tinkle.

He thought it was incredibly cute that she insisted on maintaining that type of formality with him...but it wasn't necessary.

Luke wanted *all* of her.

No closed doors. No façades.

Just love.

~ *9* ~

"Think we can get a lil music going around here?"

Aris didn't look up from her sketch, but she heard Troy pad his way over to the entertainment console where his stereo lived. It wasn't long before the classic sounds of eighties and nineties R&B filled the silence.

"Thank youuu!" Aris finally looked up from her work to smile at him. "Just when I was beginning to think you were useless…you step up. Yay you."

They worked another twenty minutes, Aris bobbing her head to the music as she sketched while Troy perfected a gory gash and lacerations on a test mask. It had been a productive afternoon at his apartment, both artists playing off each other's strengths as they brainstormed and toyed around with ideas for the new contract. Though Nate wasn't around, it didn't slow their progress. His absence actually sparked a different energy between Aris and Troy, one that allowed them to really connect and maximize their complimentary talents.

When the current song ended and the piano intro to *When I Think Of You* began to play, Aris dropped her sketch pad and threw her hands up. Troy glanced at her with amusement in his eyes, watching as she sang the lyrics into the remote she snatched from the end table, enthusiastically channeling Janet…finger pop, two-step, bouncy strut and all.

Troy laughed, long and hard. "If you don't sit yo no-dancing ass down somewhere…"

Aris ignored him, singing and skipping over to the stairs. She climbed half way up and managed to slide down the banister in the same manner that the pop star had done in her video almost thirty years ago. When her legs hit the floor, Aris did a few twirls and hit Troy with some shoulder action then tilted her head all the way to the left before letting her body follow in a hilariously awkward execution of the snake.

Troy laughed harder before giving Aris a slow clap.

She clowned a little bit more until the song ended and then she collapsed on the sofa next to Troy. "Damn! Done lost *all* my breath. I gotta do better."

"Janet would be proud, baby doll." His eyes slowly swept her body before settling on her face. "Water? I'm guessing you need it…being so out of shape and all."

Aris flipped him off with a sweet smile.

"Happy to," Troy replied on his way to the kitchen.

When he returned, there were two bottles of water in his hand. Extending one to Aris, Troy sat on the opposite end of the sofa with a curious look on his face. "Trying to recall you ever mentioning that you can actually sing."

Aris brought the bottle to her lips, took a big gulp and swallowed. "I. Can. Actually. Sing. There...it's *mentioned*. I just don't do it very often. Usually, I only sing around Luke..." She paused before her eyes shot to the clock hanging on the grey-painted wall. In a blink, she scrambled to her bag that she dropped on the kitchen bar counter right after she arrived.

She checked her phone.

The light was blinking.

Smiling, she checked the text messages Luke left and began bouncing around.

"Mr. Wonderful, I presume?"

Aris pressed her phone against her chest and sighed happily. "Yes! And he's taking me out." She grabbed her bag and rushed back into the room to clean up her mess. "So...buh-bye."

"Nah. We're not done here. Dreamboat has to wait."

"You got it. Text me later if you get stuck again. I can finish the rest of my part once I get home." She slipped her arms into her jacket. "I'm late for my date."

Troy rose from the sofa and walked Aris out of his apartment to her car. When she unlocked the door with her wireless key fob, he held the door open until she climbed in and got settled. After pushing it closed, Troy made a few circles in the air and Aris rolled down her window in response.

Noticing his foul mood, she shook her head. "Seriously? It's not like it's due next week. I'll be back tomorrow. Promise."

"Answer your phone. I might need you later."

"I will if I'm not getting busy."

Troy frowned and Aris laughed as she started grinding into her driver's seat. "Later man."

"Be safe, baby doll."

She winked. "Always."

Luke's gaze dropped to the watch on his wrist.

As the seconds ticked by, he tried not to overreact.

Running a hand down his face, his hand stopped just over his mouth. The television was on, but he had no idea what the news anchor was talking about. From the looks of the images, it was another smash and grab in Buckhead. Or maybe near Perimeter.

He honestly didn't care.

What he really wanted to know was where Aris was.

It was her idea to go out for the evening. Date night, she'd said to him before leaving the house. He was all about that, preferring a romantic night out but figured that after working all day that she may want a more casual evening, maybe do an easy dinner and catch that Marvel movie she mentioned last week.

He didn't care what they did tonight.

He just needed to be close to her.

Right. Now.

Luke had already suppressed his irritation once when she text him back saying she was "running a little behind"...whatever that really meant. Aris had been gone for the past five hours, well over the three she estimated. How long did it really take to paint masks and draw some damn sketches?

Luke was still in his head when Aris strolled through the front door with no worries. She rushed right toward him, her eyes bright, her smile for him. Without a word, she planted the sweetest kiss on his lips and told him how happy she was to see him.

And just like that, Luke's irritation dissolved.

It no longer mattered.

Aris was here now.

With him.

After some deep kissing and heavy petting, they left home for a steakhouse on the east side. They rode in comfortable silence as Luke drove, Aris's left hand in his right one, both resting in her lap.

"Troy's going to finish up everything and send me the final version later tonight," she said, finally breaking the silence. "We handled most of the grunt work. He's got it from here."

"Aris saves the day again, huh?"

"Damn right." She smiled brightly. "What would he do without me?"

Luke didn't respond.

Instead, he listened as Aris continued to talk about her time with Troy the rest of the way to the restaurant, and during dinner. When dessert arrived, she paused and tilted her head, looking at him curiously. "You're bored to tears, aren't you?" She giggled. "Now you know how I feel during those dry-ass business dinners you make me sit through." She winked. "So...we're finally even."

Eyes cast down, Luke kept slicing his steak.

"You're in a place."

Responding to her words, Luke caught Aris's gaze. It

was their code, what they said to each other to acknowledge when something was wrong and the offended partner was not pressed to discuss the matter although it was definitely noticed by the other.

Aris sipped her water and began to eat.

Waiting.

Tired of the silence, Luke sat back in his chair. "I'm fine, Moody. Just enjoying our night out...just the three of us."

Aris knitted her brows. "What? Three of us?"

"You, me...and Troy." He kept his eyes locked on hers. "Maybe we should call him. As much as you're talking about him, he might as well join us in person."

Luke knew he pressed a button when her nose flared. He expected a smart remark, but she remained calm. And quiet. He didn't know what to make of that.

"Don't do this," Aris finally said.

Luke turned to flag the server. "Check, please."

Silence covered them and they left the restaurant. Aris slipped her hand in his and smiled up at him in an attempt to ease the tension. No words. Just silly facial expressions until she finally got him to smile. When they were inside Luke's car, she leaned over and kissed him. A sweet kiss like the one she gave him when she got home earlier.

And just like that, his irritation dissolved again.

They made it to the movie theater on time, but Luke was completely distracted. He hadn't meant to let this whole Troy situation get the better of him but this shit was pissing him off. Before long, Luke was back in his funk, making snide comments and ruining the rest of the night.

And that pissed him off more.

Because when the fuck had he become *that* guy?

The one who started shit and wouldn't let it go. The one who worried about things that didn't matter.

But it *did* matter.

Because Luke was beginning to realize something that he didn't want to admit to himself, let alone share with Aris.

He didn't trust her.

After the movie ended, Luke drove them home. The car ride was so silent that he was forced to turn on the radio for some noise to distract him from what was really going on between them...what was really going on with him.

When the commercials ended, an old-school Janet song began to play and Aris suddenly began to sing. Luke glanced at her. She was bopping her head, snapping her fingers...and smiling.

"When I think of youuu... baaa-by... nothing else seems to maaat-ter..."

After the song ended, she stopped singing.

And they rode the rest of the way home in silence.

Not knowing how to resolve the rift he caused, Luke parked in the garage and watched as she entered the house without looking back. When he found her in their bedroom, she headed straight into the bathroom and closed the door behind her.

Luke pulled a rough hand down his face.

What a difference twenty-four hours could make.

This time last night, they were standing underneath the water, his mouth on her neck and finger on her clit as she moaned in his ear.

Now…this.

When she emerged from the shower, she dried off and slipped beneath the sheets. Still no words.

Luke remained silent as well and followed Aris's routine, emerging from the bathroom about twenty minutes later. He slid between the sheets, unsure of whether or not to speak. Instead, he inched closer to her naked body and waited.

She scooted back just a little.

Enough for him to know that it was okay to touch her, to hold her…yet she still had no more words or time for him.

Fair enough.

Luke closed his eyes and was asleep in minutes. He dreamed of them walking along the beach. Where…he wasn't sure. Aris was smiling at him and it made his chest tighten. She crooked her finger at him, telling him to come closer. As the ocean breeze flipped her hair, he dipped his head and tasted her lips…

Luke's eyes opened.

Turning his head, he noticed that it was almost three a.m. and that Aris was gone.

Throwing back the sheets, he sat up and pushed himself off the bed. When he stepped out of the bedroom, he followed the light…

And found a mess in the family room.

Aris in the middle of it, as usual.

Leaning against the wall, he watched silently as she worked, still regretting his earlier rant about Troy during dinner. Something about that dude still rubbed Luke the wrong way, but he had to find a better way of expressing himself to Aris about it.

"You may as well sit down…"

Aris hadn't even turned away from her work.

Luke smiled.

She could always sense his presence without him having to say one word.

Rubbing the back of his neck, Luke took a deep breath and made his way to the sofa. He braced his elbows on his knees and leaned forward, a serious look on his face. "Moody, I—"

"Shut up."

He tried to speak again, but her eyes silenced him.

Rising from the floor, Aris stood and made her way over to him. Luke's eyes scanned her body, noticing that she was naked beneath the thin tee she was wearing. His eyes found hers again.

With a small smile, Aris straddled him and covered his mouth with hers. His hands roamed her back before cupping her ass while she rocked slowly against him, making him ache for her.

Soon, Aris's shirt and Luke's boxers were tossed and they made slow love on the sofa, against the wall, on the floor, then again on the sofa.

Luke released all his earlier frustrations and allowed Aris to do what only she could—center him.

And, as always, he found peace.

~ *10* ~

It was her favorite night of the week.

Camped out on the sofa, Aris had her snacks, drinks, phone and a fluffy blanket. She would be in this same position for the next three solid hours, and it was going to be glorious.

It was the only night of the week that she ever had time to catch up on her tv shows. Her DVR was three percent from capacity and she had much more than three hours of television to watch, but tonight, she would be able to get it in.

Tonight was her "me" time.

Luke was out with Devin somewhere and she was secretly happy about it. Not that she didn't miss him, but she had definitely missed her time to only be concerned with herself and what she wanted to do. That all went out of the door the moment they moved into the house a few weeks ago. Not that she didn't like their new place, she actually loved it, especially the extra space it provided — an open interior and spacious floor plan; expansive windows; custom, island kitchen next to a sunken family room with a massive, multi-shelf, floor-to-ceiling media center; two en-suite bedrooms; and a master suite with an adjoining sitting room and French doors that opened to a private balcony showcasing perfect views of the ground level deck and level, lush lawn surrounded by lots and lots of trees.

It was unbelievable, especially when she saw it for the first time.

Her initial thought had been financial, but Luke smiled his easy smile and told her not to fret, that they could afford it. He kissed her before she frowned, before she could remind him that he was once again using the wrong personal pronoun given the current balance in her bank account. That kiss sparking a smile, prompting positivity that elicited excitement.

She had never lived in a house this grand.

And now she would…because of Luke.

Aris rode that thrill until the key was in her hand. After that, there was no time for emotions. It had been a whirlwind for them to finish packing, start moving and get settled all while maintaining their hectic work schedules. Even now, she still had some apprehension. Not that she wasn't used to being with Luke, it was just that this all-inclusive experience was much different than when she was simply spending some nights and weekends at his old apartment or he at hers.

Now, this was her home.

She couldn't run away to her apartment when she

needed space or a break from the pressure of having to be "present" all of the time with him—morning, noon and night.

It was exhausting.

Maybe part of it was the jolt of change and the general newness of truly living together. She wasn't quite sure how that was supposed to work. Having lived alone for years, Aris had become used to existing without expectations at home. When you wake up every morning and walk out the front door, the world demands you to turn up each and every second. Home had always been her refuge, her time to be whatever she needed to be, to not give a shit about pleasing anyone but herself.

That sacred time to herself always looked different, depending on the kind of day she had. Today, in particular, required that she strip down to her panties, gather snacks and a bottle of rum, then camp out on the sofa and snuggle under a blanket to watch a few hours of some pretty damn good television shows.

Usually, she would turn her phone of as well.

Today, it was on vibrate and within arm's reach.

Because Luke was a constant communicator.

Aris glanced at the phone. It hadn't rung or buzzed since he left about an hour ago. She hadn't begun her three-hour television marathon just yet, too busy gathering her goodies and preparing her own personal deserted island that was the sofa. Luke had simply smiled at her, no words. He let her be. Probably sensing that she needed this time, which is why he so graciously told her that he was going to watch a game with Devin and that he would be back later that night.

He didn't give an exact time.

And she didn't ask for one.

Still, her eyes darted to the screen of her phone ever so often, anticipating that it would light up at any moment with Luke's face or buzz loudly with his message.

That he might need her.

She'd never been needed before.

Scratch that, she probably had but didn't really give a damn about things like that at the time.

But now, she gave the most damns ever.

And, truth be told...

She was secretly thrilled about that too.

Luke returned right before midnight.

Aris was knocked out on the sofa, her tv binge still going on without her.

He sat on the edge of the sofa, watching her. She wasn't snoring, which surprised him. Her chest was rising and falling in a slow, even rhythm and her face looked as peaceful as he had ever seen it.

Reaching out, he fingered a strand of her hair before moving it away from her face. He wanted to move her, from the sofa to the bed, but she looked so comfortable that he decided not to disturb her. A fleeting thought of him joining her, lifting her up and pulling her body against him, letting her wrap her limbs around him and place her head on his chest was strong in his mind, but he resisted.

Instead, he stood and gave her one last look.
She needed this time.
Her "me" time that she never asked him for.
So he kissed her face, walked away…and let her be.

~ 11 ~
OCTOBER

Buuuzzz.

Aris and Troy stopped working, their heads turning to search for their phones. Both buzzed once, signaling a message. Troy ignored his, but Aris stood and crossed the room to answer hers.

"It's Nate," Aris announced. "Says he's stuck."

Troy shook his head and kept working.

Aris pressed the phone icon on the screen.

Nate answered immediately.

"You suck. We've been waiting on you an hour."

"Man..." Nate released a frustrated sigh. "Selah's still shopping. Y'all need to come through, give me an out."

"Negative." Aris pressed the speaker button, so Troy could listen and join in the conversation. "Tell Selah I said hello and to break the bank."

Troy and Aris listened as Nate droned on and on, building a case for them to meet in Central Park and take advantage of the nearly eighty-degree weather day. He pitched the benefits of maximizing time by meeting him now instead of waiting for him to get there later and the value of what would be their generous donation to his joint emotional bank account with Selah, how with a simple shift in location and a gallon of gas, it would be a win-win for them all.

Aris laughed and Troy shook his head again.

"Emotional bank account?" I asked, confused.

"I've been making too many withdrawals lately and she's been on my ass about it...thus, shopping," Nate explained. "She's checked off everything on her list, but it's like she's stopping at every random store in this bitch just to fuck with me or some shit."

"Aww, I admire your commitment." Aris turned to Troy, amused. "Gotta go save the homie. I'll drive."

"Hell nah," Troy finally said, a frown on his face. "We're already comfortable. Take your balls out of the bag you just bought her...we'll see you here in thirty."

Laughing, Aris took the phone off speaker and pressed it to her ear. "Let me speak to Selah."

When Selah said hello, Aris made her plea to steal Nate for about an hour and promised to return him. She made it seem like it was all her idea, which saved Nate and lessened the likelihood of Selah saying no. Aris had every confidence that it would work and it did. But what she didn't expect was Selah's invitation to catch a movie right after their meeting was over.

"Sounds great," Aris replied. "See you soon!"

She ended the call and began grabbing her stuff, practically feeling Troy's disapproval. Ignoring him, she waited until he finally stood from the sofa, grabbed his stuff and followed her out of his apartment.

"Stop being such a grouch, Troy. I think it's cute how much Nate is trying to make it work with Selah. It's not easy to keep a significant other with our schedules and the work that we do." Aris glanced at him and smiled brightly. "Besides, it's a gorgeous day to play outside."

Troy shrugged.

"Oh, and Selah invited us to see a movie with them when we're done. I told her it was cool."

"A stop in Central Park and a double date too?" Troy replied, flatly. "Outstanding."

"That's the spirit." Aris raised her hand. "High five!"

Troy grinned. "You are so damn silly. Keep your eyes on the road and take this next exit."

Aris stuck out her tongue and crossed three lanes of traffic. "I know where I'm going."

They arrived at Atlantic Station twenty minutes later. Instead of parallel parking on the street near Central Park, Aris proceeded to the underground parking deck. It wasn't long before they were strolling on the sidewalk between Strip and Rosa Mexicana, searching for Nate, who they found sitting alone at a rectangular mesh top table near the grassy area dotted with kids and seven, young, flexible women positioned on colorful mats in a downward dog pose, their impressive asses pushed up high towards the cloudless blue sky.

Troy slowed his stroll to observe the yoga group while Aris snuck up on Nate.

"Boo," she said before grabbing his shoulders.

Nate turned his head and yanked his earbuds. When he saw it was Aris, he grinned. "Man…you were about to get slammed for real. You know better than to roll up unannounced." Nate looked behind and around her. "Troy's hatin' ass stayed behind?"

Aris laughed. "He's here…but you know he had to stop and enjoy the view." She pointed to the yoga group and several men who had also turned their head to check out the eye candy. "Those chicks got quite a few fans out here."

Nate turned his attention back to his work. "I guess."

"You guess, huh?" Aris pressed both of her hands, one over the other, to her chest. "Because you only have eyes for Selah, now. I am loving this new version of you, Nate. You are too cute."

"You are too whipped," Troy added, appearing out of nowhere to sit the empty chair that offered the best view of the women.

"It's a matter of perspective, bruh," Nate responded sarcastically before he slapped hands with Troy in greeting. "I'd take whipped any day…your lonely ass should try it sometimes."

Aris and Nate laughed hard while Troy scowled.

"Single but never lonely, dude," Troy replied, his signature smirk returning when he turned his head to gaze at Aris. "When it gets too rough, I still got Baby Doll to keep me company."

"You wish," Aris said, twisting her lips.

"Indeed," Troy replied, smirk to smile.

Nate raised an eyebrow at the exchange but Aris ignored it and proceeded to kick off their meeting. For the next hour, they shared updates on their current projects, resolved impediments, discussed next steps and strategized a new contract that Nate recently landed and invited them to work on with him.

Halfway through the meeting, Selah stopped by and distributed warm hugs to us all before she dropped off more shopping bags and rushed off to attack more stores. Nate grimaced when she walked away and Aris simply patted his hand and laughed while Troy shook his head in disappointment.

Once the trio's work was done and Selah's purchases were secured in the trunk of Nate's SUV, the four friends wandered through the streets, wasting time until the movie started. While Selah engaged Troy in an animated explanation of why one of her girlfriends would be a perfect match for him, Nate slowed his pace to fall in step with Aris who was trailing behind them, the shades on her face protecting her eyes as she gazed up at the sky.

"What're you doing?"

"Enjoying this beautiful day." She looked at Nate and smiled. "This was a great idea. Win-win for real." Nate continued to stare at her, and Aris began to feel as if she was missing something. "What?"

"Troy," he clarified. "Last I checked, you and Luke were solid, but lately Troy has been pushing up and I don't know…it's like you don't seem to mind."

Confused, Aris wrinkled her nose. Troy and Selah were several steps ahead, but Aris followed Nate's lead and kept her voice down when she finally found her words. "Me and Luke are as great as you and Selah… and Troy is just being Troy. You know that."

"What I know is that he's feelin' you. He always has. You know that too. So what're you doing?"

"Nothing," Aris insisted. "Nate, come on." She laughed but stopped when his expression remained unchanged. "Are you serious? You of all people should definitely know there's nothing going on between me and Troy, so what the hell are you really getting at?"

"That's my point. I'm with y'all more than anybody and it's blatantly obvious to me, so it won't be long before others start to pick up on it too...namely, Luke."

Aris thought back to her conversation with Luke, but she refused to give Nate the satisfaction of confirming his conclusions.

"Look, I'm not tryin' to get in your business...I'm just being a friend. And, as a friend, I'm just trying to help you avoid the drama I experienced with Selah a few months ago about Deidre. We almost broke up over all that shit."

Aris nodded, remembering the hair stylist on set that took a stalkerish interest in Nate, to the point that she began interrupting his progress with Selah. "Whatever happened to Deidre anyway? I heard she got a gig in Miami. Y'all still talk?"

"Hell nah," Nate responded immediately. "After she posted them damn cropped pics of me and her on social media, like we were on a date or some shit instead of out celebrating with the rest of the crew, I told her ass to step. Unfriended, deleted number, all that. Ain't spoke to her since. Don't want to either."

"Wow. But that was on Deidre. It wasn't your fault."

"Yeah, it was on her, but I shouldn't have let it go that far." His gaze fell on Selah, still several feet ahead of them, walking and talking with Troy. "It took me almost losing her to realize some shit ain't worth the trouble. So now, ain't nobody jumping over Selah, in any way…which is why I had to damn near beg y'all to meet me down here. I'm still trying to get back in the black for that mishap."

"Emotional bank account?"

Nate nodded. "Emotional bank account."

"I hear what you're saying, Nate, but Troy is not Deidre…and ain't nobody jumping over Luke either. Ever. I got this."

"Cool, then it's my bad. I just want to see you and Luke make it. Don't ever let no unnecessary bullshit mess up your future. Trust me, the payback is a bitch."

Aris laughed and hugged Nate just as Selah turned and smiled at them, waving Aris over to help her choose the movie.

"I want you and Selah make it too, Nate. You two are really great together. I'm happy for you."

Nate nodded and stuck his hands in his jeans pockets as Troy approached them. "Now if we can just find Troy's lonely ass a good woman, we'll all be straight."

Troy frowned. "What the fuck? First, Selah trying to push her girl off on me and now y'all over here on the same bullshit too?"

"Actually, I met Carla about a week ago, dude…she's hot *and* she can cook her ass off. Don't miss out."

"Fuck yo sales pitch, Nate. I'm good."

Aris walked away to join Selah, laughing as Troy and Nate continued their bickering.

Luke was getting tired of all the schmoozing.

Tonight had been yet another night of elbow-rubbing and networking, this time at the home of an industry titan whose parties were notoriously invitation-only affairs. So when Devin called and said they were on the exclusive guest list, Luke was ready to go. A few hours later, he was en route to meet him and Jessica there. Aris was out with her work crew on the south side, so he texted her that he would try to make it home before midnight.

She still hadn't responded.

Luke hadn't thought much of that until now, cruising down the highway on his way home. The house was still a work in progress with a few unpacked boxes here and there, but it felt more like home than anywhere else he'd ever lived except for his childhood home in Savannah.

Aris had everything to do with that fact.

As much as she initially fought him at first about living together, it pleased him to see how consumed Aris had been with settling in and "making them comfortable." Her words, delivered with her signature smile the first night they spent together in the house. From then on, Luke had given Aris free reign with everything except the bedroom they shared for fear that he would come home after work one day and walk into the master suite to see a damn bird cage hammock suspended from the ceiling or some shit. As much as Luke loved her creativity, he had his limits.

Switching lanes, Luke thought about how impatient he was to come home to Aris every evening, how eager he was to wake up with her every morning and go to bed with her every night. How it was getting more and more difficult for him to actually remember a time when he didn't love and desire her. How she had become as necessary to him as breathing. How he was certain that his life would never be as vibrant and fulfilling without her.

Exiting the highway, Luke slowed to a stop at a red light. Instead of music, he'd opted for silence during his ride home. The entire evening had been a bunch of chatter so Luke was happy to finally be alone with his thoughts. Naturally, Aris was the first on his mind. Missing her was his default. He couldn't wait to get home after having the spent the entire day away.

On impulse, he called her again.

No answer.

He left a voicemail message then hung up.

When his thoughts began to shift into dangerous territory, Luke dialed Devin. Told him that he changed his mind and would meet him at their friend's house for the fight party tonight. After hanging up, Luke didn't question his decision to bypass home. True, the last thing he was in the mood for was more people, but going home to an empty house would only keep his mind preoccupied with the wrong things.

Luke arrived at the party about thirty minutes later and stayed until well after midnight. The fight was what it was, but the party itself was cool. Old college friends that Luke hadn't seen in a while, friends that he would couldn't wait to introduce to Aris one day soon.

His phone buzzed.

Checking the screen, Luke saw it was a message.

It was from Jessica. She was sharing exciting news about a connection she made earlier at the party and even better news about arranging a business dinner in the coming week to gauge the interest level.

Luke replied yes.

Still no response from Aris.

Exhausted after the fight party, he drove home. Aris was still out, so he text her and fell asleep on the sofa waiting for her to walk through the door or, at the very least, let him know that she was okay.

A few hours later, the land line rang.

Startled awake by the sound, Luke shot up and planted his feet on the floor. It rang again, and he squinted his eyes to check his watch, more surprised that the house phone was ringing at all than how late it was. Luke and Aris never used the house phone. Most people knew to call their cells, but then again it was the middle of the night. When it rang a third time, Luke snatched the cordless phone from its base on the end table and answered.

"Hello?"

A pause.

"Hello?"

"Can you hear me?"

Aris.

Luke checked the caller ID. She was calling from a blocked number. "Yeah, baby, I can hear you. Where are you calling from and why aren't you home yet...are you all right?"

"Yes, I'm...no."

She sounded hesitant. Nervous.

It put him on edge. Made him grip the phone.

"Please come get me." Another pause. "I'm in Macon and ahh…well, we umm…we got arrested tonight on some bullshit charges and – "

"What?" Luke instantly saw red, unable to control the volume of his voice. "Who is we and what the hell were *you* doing to get caught up in that shit?"

"I'll explain later, I promise, but please…" She sighed heavily into the phone. "Please just come get me."

Luke checked the clock again as Aris told him exactly where she was being held. It was now 3:08AM. He felt the anger and confusion building, but his mind could only register the fear he heard in her voice. That alone made him dial back his emotions, his only concern now to get to her. "I'm on my way."

~ 12 ~

They were avoiding each other.

Aris woke first and stared at the whirling ceiling fan after another pitiful attempt at sleeping, reflecting on last night's nightmarish events that were now very much her waking reality.

After a silent ride home from the police precinct, Aris followed Luke into the house and watched him for a sign—to talk, to argue, something. He remained quiet. She took the hint and hid in the shower until her skin wrinkled, joining him in bed almost forty-five minutes later but keeping her distance, giving him space to process her arrest. The painful silence between them eventually lulled Luke to sleep, and Aris was beyond grateful for the temporary delay of their inevitable discussion, certain that he would drill her for details as soon as he opened his eyes.

The anxiety was super real.

She lay in bed motionless on the outside and restless on the inside, fully reduced to a sad, twisted guilt ball of emotions, and still at a total loss for the appropriate words to explain her poor judgment and subsequent bad decisions in a way that wouldn't come across as the dumbest shit ever.

Tired, fretful and deep in thought, Aris rewound her mental highlight reel of fails from the past twenty-four hours. Truthfully, all of it really was pretty stupid, beginning with a phone call from Kyle. She almost didn't hear her phone to answer it, too busy strolling around and goofing off with Troy, Nate and Selah at Atlantic Station after leaving the movie theater. When Kyle mentioned that he wanted to do a random shoot with some new models south of town and he needed her help, Aris was all ears and all in.

Kyle had extended the offer to Nate and Troy as well but Nate bowed out, already committed to plans with Selah for the evening. Troy, however, was free for the night, so he rode shotgun with Aris...

Just the two of them.

They arrived almost two hours later in Macon at a local park. After Kyle facilitated a round of quick introductions, the small group got down to business. A typical Kyle photo shoot—good times and inspiring work—on what appeared to be a typical evening.

Aris remembered reading the texts from Luke, but they were so busy that she postponed responding and, when she did get around to it, her phone died. Her intent had been to go to her car and reply to Luke while charging it for about twenty minutes but slowed her stroll when she noticed a police car in the distance.

It pulled to a perpendicular stop behind Kyle's truck and Aris's car, a seemingly passive-aggressive tactic that caused Kyle to move toward the parking lot with Troy in tow.

Aris watched as two male officers emerged from the police car and met Kyle and Troy halfway. The first few minutes appeared to be casual conversation, but then their voices rapidly escalated and Aris rushed toward the men along with the other models to find out what the hell was going on.

What happened next was a series of unwelcomed exchanges peppered with hapless misunderstandings and offensive innuendos. Apparently, Kyle had made the grave mistake of not securing a legal permit to utilize the park for his photo shoot...and of also being a "militant" black man who asked too many questions and refused to muzzle us females, kindly referred to as Kyle's "questionable harem of too-vocal, indecently-clad video girls." But, in the end, it was Troy that spurred the skirmish to new heights after asserting his intent to file a civilian complaint of harassment and misconduct which prompted an unnecessarily hostile reaction from the officers resulting in multiple arrests, impounding of vehicles and the confiscation of their camera equipment and lighting accessories.

In the name of "teaching you people a lesson."

As Aris had explained to Luke over the phone while being held at the police precinct, they had indeed been taken in on bullshit charges—trespassing in a park after dark. It turned out that Kyle did have a permit, but the fact that he couldn't produce a physical copy simply allowed them to expose the true purpose of their presence—to stress that Aris, Troy, Kyle and the models were unwanted visitors in their territory.

Aris had been ready to share all of this with Luke when he posted her bail and she was released, but his sullen expression made her reconsider and silently pray for a swift bout of laryngitis. She felt herself shrinking underneath his intense gaze, his frosty eyes both inspecting and judging her from head to toe until he finally dropped his shoulders and exhaled sharply through tight lips and flared nostrils.

He'd been worried about her.

She'd done that to him.

In that moment, her mouth opened...

But no words came out.

Because his eyes remained cold.

In the middle of the lobby of the precinct, Luke and Aris squared off for seconds that felt like hours.

Then he turned and started toward the entrance of the building, and she followed behind him in silence.

And they still hadn't spoken a word since.

That was more than ten hours ago and now Aris was wondering how much longer this silent treatment was going to last.

Evening was giving way to night and her stomach growled. Guilt and shame had robbed her ability to eat so she slept, but her hunger could no longer be denied.

She rose from the bed, careful not to disturb Luke. On her way to the bathroom, an idea to pick up take-out from their favorite restaurant came to her mind but she caught herself. Borrowing Luke's car was not an option and she wouldn't dare ask him to make a food run for her, not after everything he'd already done, including having to reschedule a couple of important business meetings so he could drive her back south to retrieve her car in the morning.

Leaving the bathroom, she pulled on an oversized tee and made her way downstairs to sit in the middle of the floor with her mannequins.

Thinking. Working.

Working. Thinking.

Her thoughts won out and she sighed at the verdict.

She was a terrible girlfriend.

Always had been...but she didn't want to be.

Luke deserved better.

He was the single best thing to ever happen to her and never asked her for much, but she consistently disappointed him at every turn.

Yet he still loved her. In spite of *her*.

Gratitude filled her heart as her stomach growled, and she blinked rapidly to calm the sting in her eyes.

"You have to do better," Aris mumbled to herself.

Picking up the phone, she ordered a pizza and some hot wings. While waiting for the food to arrive, she continued working on her mannequins, contemplating the best way to get through to Luke, testing out her approach and what she would say.

Fifty minutes later, the food arrived and she was ready to make peace.

Luke was awake now, working in one of the spare bedrooms that was now their home office. She heard him moving around about an hour ago, not too long after she began working. Her hope was that he would join her but she was certain he wouldn't.

They were still avoiding each other.

Instead, he went to work in the office. The faint sounds of the printer spitting out multiple pages of who-knows-what is what gave him away. Aris rarely used that printer or any of the items on his desk. She grinned, picturing Luke frowning when he walked in and saw the clutter on her own desk and the mess piling up right next to it.

They had no business sharing an office.

But somehow, it worked.

Of all the rooms in the house, it was the only one to that fully showcased their differences...and, to Aris, it was a thing of true beauty. There were two desks, each against opposite walls. Where Luke's "side" was all dark wood, classic decor and traditional accessories, Aris's space was what she often referred to as her "productivity pod" — unorthodox in design and vibrant in color, complete with Tetris-style shelves, rainbow-shaped activity table and a cloud-cushion bench to add a little pizzazz.

Totally yin and yang.

Aris look up at the ceiling in the direction of the office. Without pause, she abandoned her mannequins, gathered the food and climbed the stairs two at a time. Leaning against the doorframe of the office, she waited for Luke to acknowledge her. He was bobbing his head, his eyes on his laptop screen as he rapidly tapped the keyboard. She stepped closer, into his peripheral. He turned his head and pulled the buds from his ears before pushing back from the desk to swivel and face her. His eyes met hers briefly before they dropped to take in the tray of food in her hands.

"I didn't know what you were in the mood for," Aris

began as she crossed the room to set the tray on top of the faux fur bean bag near the window between their desks. At least, she tried to do that but the tray was unsteady and she kept adjusting it until Luke relieved her and placed the tray on the edge of his desk. She stepped back and twisted her hands. "Thank you."

"Thank you," he replied, gesturing to the slices of pizza and wings. "I was hungry. This is great."

"You're welcome."

Dropping her head, Aris searched her mind to recall all the words she practiced downstairs before the food was delivered, but she was suddenly at a loss on where to begin. When she looked up, Luke was staring at her. Then, he opened his arms.

Welcoming her. No questions.

Her heart swelled and she went to him, accepting his invitation and sitting on his lap.

And then it happened.

She knew exactly what to say.

"I don't know how to do this," she began, looking into his eyes. "To be a real girlfriend. I've been doing a pretty poor job of it lately...with last night being the worst of it so far. And I am so, so sorry about that."

Luke caressed her thigh and nodded, acknowledging her apology and urging her to continue.

"And so...I want to be better. Actually, I want to be great which means I have to try harder. Starting now." Aris paused, chewing on her lip as she prepared to deliver her next words. One after the other, they tumbled out, explaining the details of the past twenty-four hours, of her time away from him, of her arrest. He didn't react, only listened as she shared every detail, including everyone involved. She felt him tense at the mention of Troy but, still, he remained quiet.

"I understand how irresponsible this sounds and, though Troy wasn't the only person involved, I get your reaction just now at knowing he was there. I understand that you have an issue with him...and maybe Kyle, Nate and others I work with too...but I want you to know that you have nothing to be concerned about and, like I said before, I want to be better about the being a great girlfriend thing and making sure that, above all else, you are okay...in the same way you put your anger aside, bailed me out and made sure that I was okay." She tucked a strand of hair behind her ear and took a deep breath. "To do this, I've come up with a pretty solid plan, if you're open to it."

Luke's mouth twitched in amusement. "A plan?"

"Yes," Aris said, shifting her eyes to the plates of food that was getting colder by the minute. "I propose that we start doing more things that purposefully blend our lives...not that we haven't before, because I've been to more than my fair share of your business dinners and everything, but what I mean is that we should do a lot more of that. On both sides."

"Moody, you hate those boring dinners and events."

"That may be true," she admitted. "But I love you more. And with this being a reciprocal thing, I'll get to bore you just as much with my stuff and people too."

"Uhh...thank you?"

"You're welcome." Nodding her head in satisfaction, she smiled brightly. "It's what great girlfriends do."

"Indeed."

"And if you bring people home, I'll even cook and be

the perfect hostess…sometimes."

Unable to hold it in any longer, Luke laughed. "I appreciate all the effort and enthusiasm, baby, but don't stress yourself with the food…I can cater that."

"Whatever," Aris mumbled, jumping from his lap in a huff. "I'm getting better…"

Luke reached out and pulled her back to him, kissing her face until she was no longer miffed and full of giggles. "Yes, you sure are. But I'm guessing there's a reason why you chose to order pizza and hot wings instead of cooking, right?" Releasing her from his grasp, Luke reached over to grab a slice a pizza and take a bite. "Thanks again, baby. I was hungry as hell."

Smiling, Aris eased down to the floor in front of Luke's chair and waited as he passed her one of the small plates with a slice of pizza and a few wings. They ate while catching up on everything they hadn't said to each other since their silent treatment began.

When the food was gone, Aris leaned back on her elbows and stretched her legs. "Hey, I was thinking…"

"Oh boy…"

She stuck her tongue out. "*Somebody* has a birthday coming up and *maybe* we should celebrate it in a new way…like a Sunday football house party kind of way."

Luke raised a brow. "That *somebody* would like to know what you have done with his girlfriend because you are clearly an imposter."

"Seriously," Aris continued. "Nothing big and this could be the start of our blended existence. You could invite Devin and your cousins, of course. Even Jessica too, if you want."

Luke pinned her with a look of disbelief.

"Oh, cut it out. I'm mature. And besides, my quest to great girlfriend status requires me to adjust and accept things as they are...and I know that Jessica is as much a part of your life as Devin. So no worries. Matter of fact, feel free to invite others too. It's a good way for me to meet them and further blend. And I'll do the same and invite Nate, Troy, Kyle, Chiki and some of the others I work with too...if that's okay with you?"

"Yes, baby. I see you trying...and it's okay with me."

"Perfect!" Aris rose from the floor and grabbed the tray of empty dishes. "I'll let you get back to work. I've still got some of my own to finish up."

"I won't be long," Luke replied. "You want to get out tonight or something?"

"I want to be in bed with you."

"Ahh...my baby is back. I missed you. This new party-throwing chick takes some getting used to."

Aris laughed along with him and continued out of the room and down the stairs to the kitchen. After cleaning up, she went back to work.

About ten minutes into it, her phone rang. She grabbed it and, after seeing Kim's face flashing on the screen, she abandoned her mannequins and answered before the call went to voicemail. After enduring Kim's typical rant about Aris not calling her for almost a week, she told her friend about her work week from hell before sharing her nightmarish adventures over the past twenty-four hours. When Kim asked about Luke's reaction to everything, Aris explained the "blended lives" plan she proposed to Luke and that things were back on track for them. So much so that they both agreed to a little get together at their house for his birthday in a couple of weeks.

"I may have to catch a flight to see this fiasco in person," Kim said after laughing for a full minute.

Aris didn't respond.

Kim continued joking until she realized her friend was actually freaking out a little about it. "Come on, girl...you know I was kidding. I think it's a great idea. It's about time you both get past these issues with Jessica and Troy. It's a perfect opportunity to defuse all this unnecessary tension."

"I know. I just really hope it goes well, you know?"

"It will," Kim asserted.

"It's the only way I can think of for Luke to actually see that he has nothing to worry about. Once we're all together, he'll get those foolish ideas out of his head about Troy's intentions...plus, I'll be able to officially establish myself as Luke's woman." Aris stuttered, choking on the last word. "Oh shit...did I *actually* just say that?"

"Yes, you did, honey bun...and with conviction too." Kim replied with a laugh. "Good job. You'll be a great girlfriend yet."

~ 13 ~

In keeping with the plan, Luke texted Aris an update on a private party that he and Devin were invited to attend. She texted him back with a litany of two-hands-up emojis followed by dozens of drink images and three monkeys covering their ears, hands and mouth.

Luke replied with three letters: SMH.

When Saturday arrived, Aris was ready to put her plan into action. She was serious about this new phase of their relationship and showing to Luke how much he mattered to her. She wanted to be better, not just for him, but for herself. To prove that she was capable of commitment, capable of real love.

"Hey...can you get that?"

Her thoughts vanished at the sound of his voice. The house phone was ringing, so she stood from the sofa and followed the sound until she found the cordless phone lying on the dining room table. After reading the caller ID, she answered right away. "Devin…hey!"

They chatted for several minutes, all jokes and laughter before Luke walked into the room.

"Well, Luke just appeared," Aris spoke into the phone. "Don't forget to give me all the details about that new lounge you went to a few weeks ago. Guess we can chat about it later tonight at the party."

"Oh, you're coming?"

Devin sounded surprised at the news. Aris glanced at Luke who kissed her forehead. "Yep."

"Cool," he said casually. "I thought it was just going to be the three of us, but this is much better. Luke won't be moping all night wishing you were there because you will be. You picked a good one to attend too…the food and entertainment should definitely be top notch tonight. They spare no expense and the property itself is like a damn compound."

"Three of us?" It was far from an innocent question, her nerves on high alert from the second the revelation casually slipped from Devin's mouth.

"Me, Luke and Jess."

"Right. The three amigos." Aris cleared her throat and smiled, hoping it would extend to her voice. "Hold on a sec."

Passing the phone to Luke, she left the room and raced to her closet. She didn't have to look long to know that there was nothing fancy in there for her to wear. Her eyes scanned the outfit hanging on the closet door. She'd been happy with it earlier but now…it just wouldn't do anymore.

Jessica would be there.

Moving to the bathroom, Aris stared into the mirror

for several seconds before she began piling her hair atop her head and posing at awkward angles.

"You have to do better," she mumbled to herself.

Rushing back into the closet, she traded her shorts and tee for a tank, a lightweight jacket and skinny jeans. A few minutes later, she was breezing past Luke with slouch boots on her feet, bag hiked high on her shoulder and phone in hand. He was still chatting with Devin, but his eyes swept her changed appearance before he raised his brow in question.

"I'll be back," she whispered. "Errands."

"Hey, hold on a minute." Luke pulled the phone away from his ear and pressed his lips against hers in a light kiss. "Okay. Would you mind grabbing a few things for me while you're out? I'll text you a list."

"A list?" Aris ran a hand over her hair. She didn't have enough time to transform herself AND be a list-completing girlfriend too.

"It's not much." Luke grinned, noticing her twisted lips and rising level of impatience. "Don't worry about it though. I can pick it up later."

"No," she replied, exasperated by all her new great girlfriend responsibilities. "Text me, and I'll get them."

"Thanks, baby. See you later."

Checking the clock, Aris rushed out of the house. Once inside of her car, she sped down the road while trying to figure out who might be available to hook up her hair at the last minute.

Slowing to a stop at a traffic light, her eyes widened.

Kyle was doing a photo shoot today.

Checking the time on the dash, she smiled.

Chiki should be there.

Pulling out her phone, Aris sent her a text and Chiki replied quicker than she expected. They exchanged messages back and forth for several minutes before Aris was suckered into promising to do makeup for Chiki's cousin's entire wedding party in a few weeks. It wasn't exactly a fair trade off but, knowing Chiki, it could've been a lot worse.

Aris drove the twenty-five miles to Kyle's house. There were several cars in the driveway and on the street, so she parked at the curb and dashed around the house toward the basement door. Upon entering, she immediately noticed Kyle stretched out in an awkward position on the floor, talking seductively to one of the models as she struck pose after pose at his direction. Ignoring the show, Aris went in search of Chiki but stopped when she heard a familiar voice call out to her.

"Baby doll, what the hell are you doing here?" Troy asked, with a devilish smile. "Trying to upstage Ana Marie or something?"

At the sound of her name dropping from Troy's lips, Ana Marie turned and gave Aris a cool gaze before continuing her work on another model. Everyone, including Ana Marie, knew that Kyle preferred Aris's work above anyone else.

"Nah," she said, loud enough for Ana Marie to hear and relax. "I'm looking for Chiki. She still here?"

"Yeah, she went upstairs for a minute," Troy replied.

Aris took off. Halfway up the stairs, she felt a light tug on her arm and whirled around to glare its owner.

"Whoa," Troy said, removing his hand and raising them both in the air in peace. "What's with you?"

Realizing that she was on edge, Aris dropped her

shoulders and let out a long, shaky breath. "Nothing. It's..." For a moment, she felt like lightening her load but decided to keep it to herself. "It's dumb. Just got lots to do today and I'm running late and needed Chiki to hook my hair up."

"Hook your hair up?" Troy repeated in surprise. He seemed ready to laugh but must have thought better of it when she glared at him again. "Baby doll, you always look great but if you insist." Tilting his head, observing her. "Humor me though...why the sudden need to switch up?"

Aris looked away, chewing on her bottom lip.

"Ahh. Dreamboat strikes again."

She ignored the sarcasm in his tone and ran a hand over the reason for her unexpected visit. "Whatever. I gotta find Chiki."

Aris raced up the stairs and entered the small hallway to the main level and found Chiki with a few other unfamiliar women. After quick introductions, Aris followed Chiki back downstairs to get dolled up.

"Did you at least wash it before you came?" Chiki asked as she removed the ponytail holder to inspect Aris's tangled hair.

She glanced over her shoulder. "Yeah, about that..."

"Damn, Aris..."

"I know, I know...I can wash it myself now and you can handle the rest." Chiki crossed her arms so Aris clasped her hands and laid it on extra thick. "Pleeeaaassseee...I need you in the worst way. Ain't nobody can make mane miracles like you, hunty."

Chiki's lips twitched, but she refused to smile. "Take your ass on and get started. And don't use that cheap shit...look in my bag and grab the tall purple bottles. One is a leave-in conditioner. We don't have time for anything else."

"Yay." Aris hopped up from the chair and strolled over to Chiki's bag to grab the bottles then make her way over to the makeshift salon on the other end of the fully finished basement. Inside, there was a barber's chair and two styling stations along with a hooded dryer/chair combo and mobile, double-storage service cart. Aris eyed the shampoo bowl, wondering if she should bother with the attached chair. The sink was pretty low but she was sure she duck her head under the spout without injuring her back —

"Need some help?"

Aris turned to find Troy and his signature smirk.

"Nah," she snapped. "I got this."

Removing her jacket to prevent it from getting wet, Aris revealed her flimsy tank underneath. She turned on the water and fumbled around, bending at weird angles until Troy snatched the water sprayer from her hand. "Fuck you doin'? Sit down."

She sat, eyeing him with suspicion and curiosity. He adjusted the water before pressing a firm hand on her bare shoulder, pushing her backward until her neck rested in the curve of the shampoo bowl and her hair spilled into the deep sink.

"See you don't even know what you're doing," Aris said as his fingers trailed through her tangled strands. "Where's my cape and towel?"

Troy flicked water into her face before grabbing a folded hand towel from the mobile cart and dropping it into her lap. "There's your towel."

"Still don't know what you're doing," she mumbled.

"I suffered three sisters plus my mom is a beautician so, trust me, I'm certified." He ran his hand over her hair, beginning at her forehead and following her hair to its end. "Does that meet your approval, Your Royal Pain In The Ass?"

Aris cursed him and closed her eyes. A second later, she cracked open her right eye and warned him not to fuck up. Troy flicked water into her face again, and she relaxed as the warm water flowed through her hair. Aris soon realized that Troy really did know what he was doing, releasing a dreamy sigh of satisfaction as he continued to masterfully massage her scalp.

"Mm-hmm…" Troy muttered with amusement.

Aris didn't even respond, too busy enjoying Troy's hands and being grateful that she didn't end up having to bend over this short-ass sink.

A few washes and rinses later, the water stopped.

"Sit up," he said.

Aris sat up as instructed, slightly disappointed. When Troy walked away, she blinked and smacked her lips in protest, already missing his shampoo game.

"The rest is on you."

"What kind of lazy ass beautician's son are you?" Aris yelled before Troy left her sitting alone. Grabbing the leave-in conditioner, she fingered it through her hair before following his path to the main area.

An hour later, Aris was smiling at her reflection in the mirror, her hair impressively laid. She thanked Chiki with a long, tight hug and a promise to follow up soon about the wedding details. With her bag in hand and jacket draped over her arm, Aris waved a goodbye to everyone on her way out.

Lowering his camera, Kyle glanced at her and winked. "You look fly as hell, Aris. Fucked up how you can come through for Chiki but not stick around to put in some work for me."

Aris laughed, knowing that Kyle was only slightly serious with his remark. She blew him an exaggerated kiss and turned toward the door.

"Kyle's right," Troy said, stepping into her path, purposefully blocking her exit. He reached out to finger one of her tresses and tilted his head, regarding her with brazen interest. "You're always gorgeous but now...you look unbelievable, baby doll."

Aris held Troy's gaze for a moment too long, seeing recognizing something in his eyes that was both alluring and alarming, all at once. Her tongue darted across her lips as she took a step back to distance his hand from her hair, to distance herself from him. "No touching. You're gonna mess it up." When his eyes dropped to her lips, she took another step back and assumed a playful stance with a hand on her hip in an effort to correct the sudden awkwardness in the air and restore their normal, jovial nature. "Stop being weird." Suddenly unsure of what else to say or do, she hiked her bag onto her shoulder and grinned. "You were on point with the shampoo, Troy. 'Preciate that. Just add it to my tab."

"Yeah," he said in a low voice. His eyes never wavered, but his hands disappeared into the front pockets of his jeans. "I'll collect later."

Ignoring Troy's loaded statement, Aris dashed out of the basement. Once inside her car, she checked her phone and noticed two missed calls from Luke.

"Shit."

Biting her lip, she listened to his voicemail message.

From two hours ago.

"Shit, shit, shit…"

Aris wasted no time getting to the highway. No stop at the mall to shop. She would just have to make do with the outfit still hanging on the closet door at home.

Five minutes from home, Aris rolled to a stop at a traffic light and pulled out her phone to call Luke. He answered on the second ring and asked if she'd eaten yet. Her stomach growled loudly in response. "Nope."

"When I didn't hear back from you, I took a chance and got some Hibachi. Steak and shrimp okay?"

"That's perfect. I'll be there in a sec."

"Where are you?"

"On the way," she replied, a little too quickly. "I, um, I got my hair done."

"Oh? Didn't know you had that planned today."

Because I didn't… Aris tossed her head to flip a lock of hair out of her eyes as the lies rolled off her tongue. "I didn't. It was impulse, I guess. Just wanted to try this new salon." Aris caught her reflection in the rearview mirror and quickly looked away. "No big deal. I just thought that tonight was important so I'd do more…ya know? But I ran out of time and didn't make it to the mall to find something to wear."

"It's super casual so whatever you wear will be fine. You look great in everything so don't worry about all that. I am curious about your hair though…"

"Oh, it's nothing outrageous," I clarified, managing his expectations. Not that he really had any. Luke loved her hair any way she wore it. As long as he could play in it, he was content. "I didn't color or cut it or anything too complicated, but it's nice. I think you'll love it."

"No doubt. I always love it, but it's definitely something special whenever you decided to 'do more', as you put it."

"Yeah," Aris said, waiting for the traffic light to turn green. Something in her wanted to tell Luke the whole story, but she remembered Troy wasn't winning any points with Luke lately so it was probably best to keep the details of her impromptu hair makeover to herself. "I know. See you soon."

~ 14 ~

The palatial estate of Drs. Henry and Sheila O'Hare was a gorgeous, three-level dream. Its custom design was unlike any floorplan Aris had seen before and she marveled at the dramatic terraces, entertainment stage and poolside bar/lounge along with panoramic windows, interior fountains, arched doorways and faux finishes. It was an entirely impressive display of architectural craftsmanship and decorative detailing at every turn but the library loft was by far the best room of the Alpharetta residence.

After Sheila ended their personal tour, Luke and Aris returned to the family room where most of the guests were gathered. It was there that they finally spotted Jessica and Devin, who approached them as soon as they entered. Just as she suspected, the concept of casual would forever be lost on Jessica Knox whose chic immaculate styling was difficult to ignore. The only thing left for Aris to win was in the hair category, which Aris won by a narrowest of margins, generating an immediate compliment from Jessica while they embraced in a tolerable hug.

"What's up, Hollywood?" Devin greeted her with a grin and a hug as well, one that was meant to allay her apparent jitters. Aris was grateful for his attempt to put her at ease but, after scanning the affluent crowd, she felt everything but relaxed.

Throughout the night, Luke and Devin connected her to several people who seemed much cooler than their outward appearance would have had her to initially believe. Jessica joined their efforts as well, introducing Aris to a receptive group of classy divas and dolls who had already accomplished more in their short lives than any other women she had ever met. Though Jessica and her friends did their best to pull her into their lively discussion, Aris gradually fell silent when the conversation began to shift toward corporate office politics, sorority drama and luxury label debates. After a dutiful twenty minutes, she excused herself and drifted around until she was surprisingly summoned by Sheila O'Hare herself and promptly introduced to two ladies who peered at Aris with genuine interest.

After Sheila departed to welcome new guests, the insufferable "so what do you do" question surfaced almost immediately and Aris quickly learned that one woman was an Executive Administrative Assistant to the Dean of a Top 20 Business School and the other a First Lady of a popular metro-area pastor. Though their notable titles would suggest otherwise, the classy, spirited ladies were a real hoot. Both were fascinated with Aris's work and she cackled when the First Lady expressed how much she loved "that zombie show" and started gossiping about its starring cast members.

In the middle of a round of laughter, Luke appeared and dropped a kiss on Aris's forehead before turning a disarming smile to her new companions.

"I'm not sure if we've met," he said, extending his hand in greeting. "I'm Luke Donovan, the guy lucky enough to call this beautiful woman my lady." He looked down to stare adoringly at Aris then returned his gaze to the women.

The Admin gawked while the First Lady slipped her hand in Luke's and smiled graciously. "It's my pleasure to meet you, Luke. I'm Colleen Edwards. You did very well with Aris…she is indeed delightful."

"And I'm Kiva Burke." She shook his hand and smiled with her eyes before roping Luke into an extended conversation until he finally excused himself to chat with a few other guests.

"*That's* your man, Aris?" Kiva asked, openly ogling Luke as he walked away. "Damn, honey. High five."

Colleen laughed and Aris grinned and sipped her wine, always proud of the fact that Luke was, in fact, her man. "Yep. He's definitely mine and even better than he looks."

The women burst into rounds of giggles until Kiva noticed Jessica approach and get cozy with Luke. "So if he's really yours…who is she to him?"

"Pardon?" Aris asked, turning her gaze back to Luke and noticing Jessica perfectly poised and positioned next to him. "Oh, that's Jessica Knox—"

"I know *who* she is," Kiva commented easily. "Who

doesn't know Jessica Knox? What I'm trying to figure out is why is she so comfortable with *your* man?"

Aris peered again and noticed Jessica's hand resting comfortably on Luke's arm as the pair shared a laugh and continued talking to their captive audience.

"They uhh..." She turned away to face the women. "They dated for a while in college and shortly after. Now, they're business partners...and good friends."

"Hmph," Kiva replied, sipping her wine to hide her twisted lips.

"Stop being messy," Colleen snapped. "Excuse Kiva, Aris. She has a terrible habit of always searching for foolishness where none exists."

Noticing the sudden discomfort in Aris, the First Lady changed the subject and the Admin eventually let it go although the young woman's eyes continued to rest on Jessica and Luke until the dazzling duo moved away and disappeared out onto the patio.

Kiva shot her a knowing glance but Aris ignored it, excusing herself from the ladies to drift toward the kitchen in search of another stiff drink. Just that quickly, she regretted how much she'd shared with them and silently scolded herself. The uncharacteristic openness was nothing but the result of the alcohol she'd been consuming all night, not to mention her secret relief at managing to survive tonight without Luke for more than ten minutes when she was almost certain her fate of feeling like an alien was basically a foregone conclusion.

Glancing at the patio door, Aris ventured outside and found Luke among a group of men...sans Jessica.

A rush of air escaped her lungs.

Luke spotted Aris shortly after and waved her over. She smiled brightly and glided over to him, placing a hand on his arm just as she'd just seen Jessica do, hoping to appear sophisticated to his peers. Luke immediately slipped his arm around her waist, pulling Aris close to kiss her temple before introductions were made. Her heart swelled at his natural response to her presence, something inside her completely satisfied with the noticeable difference in how he responded to her versus the curious interaction that Colleen and Kiva had witnessed earlier with Jessica.

As the men casually discussed and debated things she knew nothing about, Aris fought to silence the troubling thoughts taking over her mind, all in stark contrast to the delightful smile she maintained on her perfectly made-up face.

Her sudden diffidence was suffocating.

Aris versus Jessica…Jessica versus Aris…

Would it always be a competition?

…briiing…briiing…

Luke glanced at the in-dash, touch screen monitor.

Jessica was calling.

Without pause, he released Aris's hand and pressed the button on the steering wheel to allow Jessica's voice to fill the cabin of his car. The two chatted about the events of the night that Aris had no knowledge of because she was spend most of her time with Colleen and Kiva at the party. Luke was glad that Aris could hear it now while he discussed it openly with Jessica via Bluetooth. He'd been wanting to share all the details with Aris, but she'd been in a funk since they left the O'Hare estate so he decided to wait her out.

After Luke bade Jessica a good night and ended the call, he turned to look at Aris. Her eyes were closed, but he was pretty certain that she wasn't sleeping and had heard every word of the conversation.

Accepting Aris's passive-aggressive behavior, Luke threaded his fingers through hers and brought her hand to his lips.

Still, she ignored him.

Lowering their joined hands to her lap, Luke trained his eyes on the highway and left Aris to her thoughts. He concluded that the party must have drained her and maybe she needed to decompress during their long ride home. Aris never did like his engagements but, like always, she suffered them for him.

After several miles, she shifted in the seat, pulling her hand from his grasp as her dress hiked up her thigh. With his now-free hand, Luke blindly trailed a finger along the hem of the dress and slipped it underneath to touch her bare skin.

"Cut it out," Aris mumbled.

"You done fake sleeping?" he asked, amused.

She didn't respond so he continued his exploration.

She shifted again and swatted his hand away. "Both hands on the steering wheel."

"I can multitask."

She turned to grin at him. He could tell that a smart ass comment was on the tip of her tongue, cued for rapid released, but it was suddenly interrupted by a loud buzzing sound. She peered down at her bag lying near her feet on the floor of the car before lifting her gaze to him.

"Multitask?" Aris smirked and playfully narrowed her eyes at him as her phone buzzed again and again. "So just fuck my life, huh?"

"You're the one looking all good with your dress hiked up," Luke replied with ease. "What did you expect to happen?"

Before she could respond, a long, drawn-out buzz interrupted them once again.

Luke's eyes shifted to the floor. "Need to get that?"

Shrugging her shoulders, Aris reached into her bag and pulled out her phone. After tapping the screen and briefly scanning it, she placed the phone inside a zippered compartment of her bag and dropped it to the floor. She angled her body toward Luke and grabbed his hand, linking their fingers once again.

"No," she finally replied.

Nothing more, nothing less.

They rode in silence for a few minutes before Luke's eyes shifted to the digital clock on the dash. "You sure? Must be pretty important for someone to be calling you this late."

Aris shrugged and closed her eyes, her head pressing against the headrest. Her unwillingness to explain disturbed him, so he glanced at her, holding her gaze.

"Eyes on the road, mister." She shifted again as Luke did as she asked. "That was Troy. He and Nate are working tonight and they probably got stuck and want to talk it out or something. I don't know."

"Why not check his message and find out?"

Aris hesitated again before a dramatic groan escaped her mouth. "So I can hear how badly they're probably fucking up my concept right now? Hell no. I don't feel like being pissed off. I'll deal with all that tomorrow."

Luke grunted in response, grinding his teeth as he considered her words and fought to control himself.

He didn't feel like being pissed off either...

But he was now.

As much as he wanted to challenge her on Troy feeling comfortable enough to call her this late—and more importantly, Aris not checking dude about it— Luke decided to shut down to prevent an unnecessary argument. They'd been having too many of those lately and Luke's intent for the rest of their night did not include them warring with each other, especially about something as insignificant as Troy.

"So what? You're mad at me again?"

Reacting to her insolent tone, Luke kept his gaze on the road. "Should I be?"

"About as mad as I should be at you yucking it up with Jessica a few minutes ago...*after midnight*."

Luke shook his head, refusing to look at Aris or engage her in the fight she was initiating...all while being shady as hell about Troy calling. "Well, the difference between me and you, sweetheart, is that I answered my phone."

"Seriously?" she asked haughtily before snatching her hand from his grasp and turning her whole body away from him to look out of the window.

Luke blew out a frustrated breath.

So much for his initial intent.

He'd done exactly what he'd been trying not to do—

engage her in the fight she seemed to have been spoiling for since they left the O'Hare estate. Deep down, Luke somehow knew that Troy was the caller before he asked and prompted Aris to square off with him. He'd been hoping to be wrong, that she would say it was Kim, Deena...shit, *anybody* but that asshole.

But his intuition had been on point.

And instead of answering the phone to quell Luke's rising suspicion of the nature of her relationship with Troy, Aris chose to be shady and pick a fight.

The fuck?

Returning his eyes to the road, Luke used his once-again free hand to activate the stereo and drown out the drama, retreating further into himself in another desperate attempt to chill and pretend not to notice the sudden churning in his gut.

~ 15 ~

Aris stormed into the house, fueled by remorse and rage, the latter emotion being the unmistakable result of Troy's audacity to call her after midnight—after she had pointedly asked him not to.

And now here she was, pacing the kitchen floor and drowning in a seemingly bottomless pit of guilt after senselessly using Luke as a convenient target for her displaced anger and annoyance.

Aris had every intention of explaining the why of the late phone call in further detail to put an end to Luke's apparent suspicions, but then he had to come at her with the Troy insinuations...again.

How many damn times would she have to tell Luke he had nothing to worry about?

Staring at the door to the garage that she left open for whenever his simple ass decided to get out of the car and come inside, Aris stopped pacing and waited.

How dare Luke trip about Troy when he had *his ex* on speaker phone, chatting and laughing with Jessica like his live-in-and-sometimes-great girlfriend wasn't right there next to him riding shotgun?

As she heard his footsteps, her mind clouded over with more imaginative thoughts of the dazzling duo together, all cheeky grins and personal space violations as they embarked on a bourgeois black Barbie-and-Ken quest to charm and rule the entire galaxy while Aris stood idly by, watching it happen like the non-factor that Luke and Jessica apparently believed she was.

Reaching for a bottle of Grey Goose, Aris popped the cork and took a generous swig. She glared at the open door, wholly bothered by the manufactured fact that it was somehow okay for Jessica to put her hands all over Luke in public but the minute that Troy happens to call her phone after midnight, Luke is suddenly dropping a red flag and calling for instant replays and shit?

She grabbed a glass and poured a double shot.

Fuck double standards.

Bringing it to her lips, Aris consumed half of the distilled liquor. As it burned its way down, another truth worked its way into her conscience, forcing her to acknowledge what she was pretending not to know.

Troy wasn't with Nate tonight.

So, Troy probably wasn't calling about work.

Which was the real reason why Aris didn't check his message...because she couldn't risk exposing her lie and allowing Luke to listen to the voicemail that Troy left for only her to hear.

Tossing back the glass, Aris finished off the shot. She braced both hands on the counter just as Luke entered and quietly shut the door behind him.

Risking a glance at his face, she saw it remained expressionless. Only his eyes registered any emotion and the chill reached her from across the room.

Luke stood incredibly still, flipping his keys around in his hand, watching her. Then his eyes shifted to take in the open bottle of Grey Goose and the empty glass on the counter in front of her. "What the fuck, Aris?"

She cringed at the formality of her name leaving his lips. Moody. Baby. Luke had a handful of pet names for her at his disposal. He never called her Aris unless he was angry, and she always hated the sound of it.

She looked him in the eyes, wanting to tell him... what? That she lied? That he was right to grill her about Troy calling so late? She wasn't prepared for that conversation or to disclose her trip to Kyle's and what happened with Troy in the basement salon which now suddenly seemed and absolutely felt very, very wrong.

Then again, it could all just be a misunderstanding.

Troy was an ass with no respect for boundaries, for sure. But Aris hadn't even checked her voicemail yet. What if Troy really was working? What if he was really stuck on a sketch or something and lost track of time and called her to talk through it?

She cursed. Her head was swimming.

Holding on to the counter, Aris focused her blurry gaze on Luke and told him the only thing she knew to be truth at that moment.

"Jessica," she finally spat out. "She's...intimidating. I, umm...when Devin called earlier and told me she would be there tonight, I-I panicked. She's better than me, in like every fucking way. So I tried. To at least make it even between me and her because we all know I'll never win. So I got my hair together and did my makeup but I didn't have time to find something chic or fabulous to wear. And I don't always say the right things because I usually don't even know what the fuck y'all are talking about most times. But Jessica does. And she's the one who always hooks you up with the right people and makes you look good in public all the time because she's...hell, she *matters*. She contributes. She always makes it happen for you. She's the reason your business is doing so great and I just...I just hang out all night in dark corners with Super-Messy Admins and the Zombie-Loving Pastor's Wives watching Jessica be better for you than I am."

The room was quiet.

Seconds went by. Felt more like hours.

Feeling exposed, Aris released a humorless chuckle and grabbed the bottle to pour another double shot. She couldn't believe all that had actually come out of her mouth. This was definitely not her finest moment, so the only thing left for her to do was to own her words and toast to that shit.

She lifted the glass to her lips and tossed it back, a little more than half disappearing into her open mouth.

After the burn, her eyes focused on the keys that stopped moving in Luke's hands because she was too drunk and humiliated to look higher and really see what he might think of her now.

"This is some pitiful shit, ain't it?" Aris laughed derisively and raised her almost empty glass high in the air. "To me...the charity case who lucked up and cuffed Mr. Luke Donovan. Cheers!"

"Stop it," Luke growled.

Aris lifted her gaze to Luke's face, expecting it to match the harshness of his tone. But it didn't. Instead, she saw confusion...and compassion.

"I'm...I'm sorry," she blurted before looking down at her hands in embarrassment. "Are you mad at me?"

Luke crossed the room, pulled the glass from her grasp and placed it on the counter. Tilting her head up, his eyes locked on hers as he buried his hand in her hair. Aris scanned his face, not a trace of anger in sight. His expression was love. All love.

"What the fuck, Moody?"

She smiled.

Dipping his head, Luke kissed her. Over and over again. Pulling away, she smiled again. Happy to hear him call her anything but Aris. "That's much better."

A grin played at his lips before his expression turned solemn. "I need you to hear me when I say there's no competition, baby. Jessica or anyone else. You don't ever have to worry about that with me. I love you."

Aris nodded, looking away.

"I love you," Luke said, earnestly. "Now. Tomorrow. Fifty years from now. It will always be you."

"How can you know that?" she asked in a whisper, fighting herself to believe him.

"Because you're my air." Luke tweaked her nose at his play on words and the intentional shortening of her name. "I can't breathe without you."

Aris began to melt at his words until the sources of his declaration registered in her mind. "No you didn't just hit me with a *Brown Sugar* and *Boomerang* remix..." Twisting her lips, she tilted her head. "Really?"

"Actually, I thought both references rather apropos."

Luke blinked, pokerfaced before his mouth relaxed into an easy smile and they laughed loud and long together, dispensing with all the drama and tension that followed them from the car into the house.

"You know you liked that shit." In a quick, swift move, Luke lifted Aris off her feet and cradled her in his arms, burying his face in her neck as he carried her to their bedroom. "But since you're actin' up, I can show you better than I can tell you."

She giggled. "I like *that*."

"Good," he said, placing her on their bed before bracing himself with both arms as he loomed over her, a predatory look in his eyes. "You 'bout to feel it too."

~ 16 ~

Aris sat forward with her elbows on her knees, cell phone in hand and turquoise thong around her ankles, frowning because her virtual opponent had just put her King in checkmate.

"Fuck," she mumbled.

Determined to win, Aris started a new game and made the first move. Seconds later, a practically-nude Luke barged into the bathroom and glanced at her before facing the mirror and turning on the faucet.

"Seriously?" Her frown returned as she sat up straighter, reaching behind her for the roll of toilet paper she forgot to secure in the tissue holder. When he didn't retreat, Aris threw the jumbo roll at his back and yelled for him to get out.

Luke dodged the attack, laughing heartily on his way back to their bedroom, leaving the bathroom door open on purpose.

Noticing the tissue that landed a few feet away from where she sat, Aris rolled her eyes. "I need the tissue!"

Luke's head appeared in the doorway. "Oh, so I'm allowed back in now?"

"Just give me the damn tissue!"

Luke grinned and strolled back inside to pick up the discarded roll before moving to stand in front of the doorway leading to where she sat. He extended his arm, presenting the toilet paper as a peace offering. "For your funky ass, my love."

She snatched the roll and scowled. "Get out!"

He shut the narrow door that closed her off to the rest of the bathroom and left her in peace. She handled her business and opened the door to see Luke had also closed the door leading to their bedroom. She locked it for good measure before stripping and stepping into the curved quadrant that was still damp from Luke's earlier shower. Ten minutes later, she emerged with a towel wrapped around her body and dripped over to the sink to brush her teeth. Just as she bent to rinse her mouth with two hands full of water, Luke knocked.

"Moody, you locked me out?"

After spitting the water from her mouth, Aris rolled her eyes then moved to unlock the door and yank it open. Luke smiled and followed her back to the double vanity where she stood in front of her sink and he stood in front of his while looking at each other in the extended mirror.

His reflection winked at hers.

Her reflection rolled its eyes and stormed out.

Aris secured her towel and dripped her way down to the kitchen. She was still sleepy, but her stomach wouldn't allow her to return to bed. Her bare feet carried her to the refrigerator where she opened the right door and removed a brand new gallon of whole milk. After placing it on the counter, she reached up to open the cabinet and blinked. Rising to her toes, she reached inside to shuffle a few colorful, half-empty boxes around on the highest shelf.

She blinked again. Then, cursed and frowned.

"Where...the...hell...are my Honey Nut Cheerios?!"

Her level of pisstivity had risen to the point of talking to herself. She slammed the cabinet door, officially convinced that this was absolutely the worst part of being boo'ed up under the same roof: putting shit up only to come back and discover it's gone.

Aris crossed her arms and leaned against the counter, her taste buds clamoring for something she couldn't have. Luke appeared minutes later, looking sinful in a tailored suit. It was almost enough for Aris to relax her posture about her missing box of morning happiness.

Almost.

She glared at him. "Where's my cereal?"

Luke's eyes widened before he ambled over with his bottom lip poked out. "Sorry, baby. I'll get some more on my way home tonight, I promise...forgive me?"

"No."

"Okay, well..." Leaning in, he pressed his lips to her neck. "Let me make it up to you..."

Luke's cologne teased her, eliciting a different kind of hunger, but Aris twisted her lips, refusing to drop the issue. "You just murdered morning for me."

He pulled back and pinned her with a pointed look. "Everything murders morning for you."

"What are you doing?" she asked, enjoying the feel of his mouth on her neck once again.

"What does it feel like I'm doing?"

She trembled in his arms. "I want my cereal."

"I can't do anything about the honey or the cheerios, but I can definitely give you the—"

Aris laughed until Luke's hand slipped beneath her towel. She waited for him to chide her about drip-drying through the house, but it never came...because he was more focused on making sure she came, lifting her onto the counter and spreading her legs, his fingers serving her morning happiness until she trembled and rained her pleasure all over his hand.

Luke kissed her nose. "Forgive me now?"

Satisfied, Aris nodded happily and reached for his belt but Luke reluctantly stopped her advances.

"Keep that buzz going for me, baby," he whispered into her ear before kissing it. "Continue this tonight."

Pouting, Aris adjusted her towel and hopped off the counter. After executing a goofy salute followed by an even goofier grin, she skipped out of the kitchen, up the stairs and down the hall into their bedroom to bury herself under the covers. Soon, Luke appeared in the doorway asking if she had seen his wristwatch. As he began searching the bedroom, Aris left the coziness of their comfy bed and disappeared into the bathroom, returning seconds later with his missing wristwatch dangling from her index finger.

"Thanks, baby...I must have left it in—"

"Yep," she replied, confirming his suspicion. "My penchant for disarray is apparently rubbing off on you, buddy. First, it's you forgetting to put your watch in your display box. Before long, you'll be mixing your towels and jeans together in the dirty clothes hamper." Aris shook her head and blew out a very well-feigned sigh of disappointment. "Damn, man...it's about to be straight anarchy up in this piece."

Fastening the watch to his left wrist, Luke's eyes swept her from head to toe. "Check you out with all these jokes before noon."

"Witticism." Aris shrugged. "A surprising side effect of morning orgasm."

"Duly noted," he said, pecking her lips.

Taking advantage, Aris slipped her tongue into his mouth and felt his smile against her lips. He conceded and kissed her back passionately for a full minute before swiftly connecting his hand with her ass.

"Later, Moody," he said, pulling away. "I promise."

"Later. Bye."

With nothing to do after Luke left for work, Aris climbed back into bed. Her first thought was to sleep given she didn't have to meet up with Troy and Nate on set until late afternoon but, after lying awake for almost forty-five minutes, she ditched the idea and grabbed the remote to watch television. The first image on the screen was of a morning talk show with a panel full of women talking about strategies for keeping the fire burning in a relationship.

Aris perked up at that and turned up the volume.

Though most of the ladies discussed the customary tasks like dressing up for your man and initiating new positions in bed, Aris was more intrigued when one of the panelists talked about the little things she did for her husband like sending sexy selfies to keep him riled throughout the day and taking purposeful breaks from each other because fire needs air to burn. When others asked for more ideas, the woman eagerly shared how she occasionally massages her husband's feet after he's had a long day. The audience began to mumble at that advice, but she laughed good-naturedly and went on to explain how the power of touch is a truly a trifecta of acceptance, adoration and appreciation, especially when extended as an act of kindness and service.

"I do foot rubs," Aris mumbled to herself as she leaned forward to absorb more of the discussion.

"When I can, I also stop by his job to do lunch and, if there's time, stick around for a quickie in his office."

The rowdy crowd roared and applauded along with the other ladies on the panel, signaling that they too have done similar things at some point in their own relationships.

When the show cut to commercial, Aris's mind was racing. The status of her great-girlfriend initiative was currently on point and under budget, having suffered no major risks or impediments — outside of her messy meltdown the other night fueled by vodka and vices — so now was definitely the time for her to level up...

And what better way to do so than by dropping by Luke's office to deliver a little afternoon delight? Her sexy, sincere and solicitous show of appreciation for the impromptu morning happiness that he so willingly and expertly bestowed upon her?

Sure, he said "later"...

But later was subjective.

And as far as she was concerned, today was as good a day as any to surprise her man with a great lunch and maybe a great time too, if he was willing.

When the show ended, Aris left the bed for the walk-in closet to remove Luke's favorite little black dress.

Yeah, she thought to herself as a slow smile stretched across her lips. *He'll definitely be willing...*

The intercom buzzed.

Luke stopped talking mid-sentence and silently questioned why he was being disturbed when he specifically indicated that he would be off-line for at least the next hour.

"Hold up," Luke said to Devin, who was seated across from him. He pressed the button on his phone to find out what would possibly make his assistant ignore his request to not be disturbed. "Whatever it is, I'll deal with it later, Renae—"

"I understand, Luke," she interrupted before he hung up. Renae had been Luke's assistant for the past six months so she was more than aware of his tendencies, especially when unnecessarily interrupted. "I'm sorry to disturb but there's a visitor here to see you—" Luke suddenly heard Aris's voice in the background, but it was too low to make out her words. "Oh. Excuse me, your...uhh...your *girlfriend*, Aris Collier is here—"

"Yes, send her in...thanks, Renae."

Luke was almost at the door when Aris pushed it open and strutted in looking surprisingly sinful. Caught up, he barely noticed the bags of food in her hands...or the indignant look on her face.

"Hey, Devin," she said after he stood from his chair. "I didn't realize you were in town, or I would have brought you some food too."

"No worries," he replied, embracing her in a warm hug. "I was about to head out for lunch anyway, so I'll leave y'all to it...good to see you, Hollywood."

Before Devin could close the door, Luke's hands were on Aris's waist. "To what do I owe all this?" He lowered his head and nuzzled the curve of her neck. "Damn. You smell incredible..."

She eased out of his arms and left him empty.

Baffled, he searched her eyes...finally noticing the wrinkle between her brows.

"She's got to go."

"Huh?" Luke almost grinned at her abrupt demand but quickly realized she wasn't joking. "Wait, who's got to go and what's happ—"

"Renae," she clarified. "Fire her."

With her bizarre words swirling in his mind, Luke stared at Aris in confusion until a thought struck him—a realization. He tilted his head and nodded slowly, regarding her with watchful eyes. "Okay."

~ 17 ~

Aris blinked in surprise, apparently expecting Luke to argue with her about asking him to fire his assistant for no apparent reason other than her desire for him to make it happen. "Okay?"

He nodded. "Okay."

She studied him. "You're not even gonna ask why?"

"No."

"You'd do it...just like that?"

"Yes. Just like that." Luke stepped closer and lifted a hand to gently press his index finger against the skin between Aris's brows until her skin smoothed and the wrinkle was gone. "I'd do that and whatever else you need me to do to help pull you out of whatever mood you may be shifting through in this moment so that you always feel safe, comfortable and secure with me."

"But...why?"

"Because it's my job to make you smile...which I'm

obviously failing at right now." Luke guided her to the small conference area of his office near the window with the best view. After she sat, he removed one of the containers from the bag and placed it on the table in front of her along with some plastic cutlery and napkins. "What else can I do for you, baby?"

"Nothing. I'm good...thank you." Aris busied herself with inserting a straw into the lid of her beverage. After taking a few sips, she finally met his gaze. "I'm sorry. I didn't...don't, umm...don't fire her. Renae. I didn't mean that. I don't want her to lose her job."

Luke sat across from her, a hint of a smile playing at his lips. "But you do want *something*...so what is it?"

Aris didn't respond right away because she didn't have a good answer. Luke blessed the food and they ate in silence as she considered his question while trying to block out her childish behavior. After careful thought, Aris finally recognized her issue with the woman...she basically catered to Luke in all the ways she had refused to...and now she had the nerve to be pissed because she just got her motivation to be better from a damn talk show and wanted to show the perky bitch that she could do it too...but better.

Aris's frown deepened.

"Quarter for your thoughts."

Aris inserted a forkful of food into her mouth and chewed energetically, causing Luke to cast her shady side-eye glances like she was a perfect candidate for a double dose of happy pills.

She swallowed her food and smiled. "Deee-licious."

"Whenever you're ready to talk, baby." Luke shook his head and began to eat. "I'm here."

"Clearly, he has a type," Aris said with an edge to her voice as she made a left onto the highway to head back home and change clothes. "Corporate, Playboy Bunny Barbies. She was like a fake ass Jessica. All the glitz...but none of the swag though."

"Girl, relax," Kim said, laughing. "You're trippin."

"I'm serious!" Aris blew out a breath as she sped down I-85. "These thirsty bitches outchea on some 'what-eva you liiiiike...' type cray. Ugh! Always ready to capitalize on every opportunity, posted up grinning and shit, ready for whatever, whenever, wherever."

"Are you done?"

"Hell nah, I ain't done!" She took a few, deep ragged breaths. "*Now* I'm done...sitting over here trying to understand what more you got to contribute to this conversation other than chuckles and giggles and shit."

"Never have I ever heard you clown quite like this," Kim said, amusement still coloring her voice. "You gotta admit this is funny as hell."

"Seriously, Kim...you 'bout three seconds from experiencing a dial tone."

"Get over yourself." She chuckled again before audibly sighing. "I don't know what's really got you going, but you need to chill. Luke loves your irrational ass, so whoever this Renae is only wishes she could be in your position...which she can't, by the way. Stop being so insecure."

That last word made Aris cringe.

There were very few things that she loathed more but

here she was enacting that shit to the extreme.

Kim laughed again. "Damn. I never thought I would see the day."

Aris frowned. "What?"

"Nothing, chick. Just happy to see my friend so in love, that's all. The good, the bad and the ugly."

They said their goodbyes and ended the call just as Aris arrived home. She disarmed the alarm and traded her little black dress for her usual garb of jeans and a graphic tee. Looking at her reflection in the mirror, she marveled at her transformation from the sexy vixen who brought Luke lunch to this version of herself that suddenly appeared a little too…ordinary.

Clearly, Aris shouldn't ever get too comfortable.

Luke had a type…one that she obviously didn't fit.

Not that it came as much of a surprise to her. Luke Donovan was traditional. The kind of man who settled down with the Jessicas of the world while the Renaes adored him from the sidelines.

She was definitely not a Jessica or a Renae.

She was anti-establishment.

An intermittent-contract-working, flip-flop-or-boot-wearing, top-shelf-liquor-drinking, sedentary-lifestyle-having, rarely-cook-but-always-dine-out diva in her own right.

WYSIWIG.

Take it or leave it.

As Aris stretched out on the sofa to watch television, her mental bravado eventually gave way to a familiar fear that Luke just may stop taking it. That, one day, he just might leave her.

Buuuzzz…

Aris reached for her phone and checked the screen.

Baby doll, I need you. Hit me up.

Tossing it aside, she closed her eyes as her thoughts shifted back to Renae and how she always controlled Aris's access to Luke. Whenever Aris called the office, Renae never failed to promptly offer to take a message. At first, Aris paid it no attention. She rarely contacted Luke while he was working and, on the occasions when she needed to reach him, she simply called or texted his phone. But the more Renae dismissed her, the more Aris accepted that she was being passive-aggressively dismissed by Luke's little assistant, who seemed to believe that he was much too busy to pause whatever he was doing to take Aris's call.

Like Luke was too important for her.

Since Renae came along several months ago, it had been consistent little digs like those that contributed to her outburst in his office. The woman never missed an opportunity to make Aris wait in line like she was some random broad trying to get Luke's attention. Much like today when she had the nerve to call Aris a visitor. Sure, this was her first time visiting Luke's office but she was no stranger, especially with her 8x10 framed photo sitting proudly on his credenza facing anyone who entered his space.

Buuuzzz...

Where you at?

Aris checked the time on her phone, wondering why

Troy was blowing her up when they weren't scheduled to meet for another two hours.

After texting back and forth, she learned that they didn't have to be on set this afternoon because the production was canceled for the next two days. She quickly checked her messages and confirmed Troy's update, surprised to see the notification sitting in inbox since noon, unopened because she'd been too busy getting glam, ordering food, bypassing an overzealous gatekeeper and sexing her man to notice.

A smile touched her lips as she recalled the last part.

Her lunch-and-little-black-dress surprise had been very well-received.

Fuck the Barbie brigade.

Aris's eyes focused on the screen as she tapped out a quick message to Luke.

I still expect later to happen, Donovan.
Afternoon happiness was an extra, not a substitute. ☺

After pressing SEND, she tapped out another.
This time to Troy.

On my way. See you in 20.

Aris pushed her pencil across the paper, bringing to life the vision in her mind earlier that morning. She would have sketched it sooner, but Luke happened and she got distracted. Most of her idea was still in her head though, and she was able to get it out as she worked quietly on the sofa in Troy's apartment. Nate sat across from her on the carpeted floor as he toyed with a few ideas of his own while Troy wasted time delivering his latest installment of his soapbox series, "Dating Is Bullshit And I Hate It."

Nate managed a perfunctory nod of support at the appropriate intervals but, after a while, Aris felt Troy's eyes traveling over to her in anticipation of some kind of response to his self-important tirade.

"Hol'up..." Aris stopped sketching and peeked under a sofa cushion expectantly before patting the pockets of her jeans several times and finally shrugging her shoulders indifferently. "Damn, man. Fresh out of fucks. Check back later though. I usually re-up after dusk."

"Your empathy knows no bounds, baby doll." Frustrated, Troy stopped pacing and collapsed on the opposite end of the sofa. "I can always count on you."

With a snort of amusement, Nate shook his head. "She's like a dude that way."

"Whatever," Aris replied, picking up her tablet to search for images. Looking at the results, she squealed in excitement and scooted closer to Troy. "Check it out," she said to him, shoving the tablet in his face.

He barely glanced. "Derivative."

"Isn't everything?" She rolled her eyes and frowned. "Stop being yourself and really look at it."

Troy grabbed the tablet from her hands and studied the screen closely. After a few beats, he passed it back to her with a slight nod. "Yeah, I can see why you're feelin' it but I had something else in mind."

Nate looked up in question. "Let me see."

The trio spent the next hour debating the overall direction of the project along with use of color and prosthetics to achieve their creation. After several rounds of arguments and Aris bullying them with her incessant opinions and inclinations, they were finally able to reach consensus.

Aris threw her hands up, wiggling in celebration.

Troy grabbed one of her arms and pulled her into a bear hug. "Anybody ever told you how much of a pain in the ass you really are, baby doll?"

"Once or twice." Aris looked up at him and smiled brightly. "But I'm always right though."

Nate laughed. "You are seriously overestimating your superpowers, buddy."

"Correction," Troy added. "A *super* pain in the ass."

"Screw y'all." She wiggled again. "I'm worth it."

Aris continued celebrating until Nate abruptly stood to stretch and announced his departure. At that, she frowned and told him they had a lot more to do.

"Selah's been blowing me up for the past hour," Nate explained as he packed up his tablet, sketchpad and pencils. "I need to get home and do the quality time."

Nate's mention of quality time pushed Luke to the forefront of Aris's cluttered mind. Reaching for her phone, she unlocked her screen and checked the notifications. One missed call and two missed texts from Luke. "It's already nine? Shit. I'm out too."

"Somebody's in trouble," Troy sang with humor in his voice. "Bye, bye, Dreamboat. Hello, Battleship."

Aris made quick work of collecting her stuff and stuffing it into her backpack. "Suck it, Troy."

"Ladies first," Troy returned, still reclining and not working on the other sofa.

"Later, children," Nate interjected before walking out of Troy's apartment.

Aris rushed behind Nate and slammed the door. By the time she climbed inside her car to start the ignition, she realized that her keys were still on Troy's kitchen counter. Jogging back up to his apartment, Aris rolled her eyes again as she almost collided with Troy in the foyer, her keys resting in the palm of his hand.

"You could've just told me you weren't ready to leave me, baby doll." He grinned as she stomped forward and snatched her keys. "Stay as long as you like. Always an open invitation for you."

Aris stuck out her tongue, ready to dismiss him when a thought surfaced. "Speaking of invitations, I never got your RSVP for the party next weekend but you're still welcome to come through. Feel free to bring a date...oh, wait. Dating is bullshit...almost forgot."

Troy shrugged.

"What about Darby? She seems cool."

"Nah. But I'll come through for a minute."

Aris shook her head. "You are so damned picky."

"If you say so, baby doll...I don't see the point in wasting my time when I know what I want."

She almost asked what his wants were out of curiosity but something in his eyes made her cancel the question. "RSVP for one, it is."

When he didn't respond, Aris opened the door and walked out, hearing Troy's voice deliver two final words before the door slammed shut.

"Open invitation."

~ *18* ~

"Touchdown!"

Several guests raised their bottled beers high in the air, celebrating a three-play, eighty-two yard drive that put the home team ahead by thirteen points. Majority of the people in the room were fans of the winning team but there were a few who were sure to remind everyone in earshot that there was still another half to play and the game wasn't over until it was over.

Aris listened from the kitchen as Luke and Devin responded to the hecklers in kind by talking much shit, generating waves of laughs and cheers. She poured a jar of salsa into a bowl and smiled, happy that the party was going so well and that Luke was enjoying himself. When she looked up and into the crowd of people, Luke's eyes were on her and he winked.

Damn if that didn't make her blush.

Kim glanced at Aris then turned her head to find the

source of her friend's smitten look. "Y'all are too cute."

Aris grinned and opened another jar of salsa.

A few minutes later, the doorbell rang and she left Kim to finish making another pitcher of margaritas while she went to open the front door. Four people said hello to her and Aris reciprocated, though she had no idea who they were. More of Luke's friends, of course...like so many others she met tonight.

Stepping aside, Aris extended her hand in welcome. "Hi, come on in. I'm—"

"Aris," she and Luke said in unison.

She whipped around, surprised to see him standing right behind her. He dropped a kiss on her lips then turned to introduce her.

"Gary, Kelly, Terri, Will...I'd like you to meet my love, Aris Collier."

Aris blushed again as the ladies gave her a hug and the men grasped her hand. Luke pointed down the hall, telling them to follow the noise. When the guests were out of view, he dipped his head and teased her neck with his tongue. She giggled and squirmed away.

"Somebody's had too many shots tonight," she said before leaning back in and stealing a kiss.

"Not nearly enough." He popped her ass with his hand and guided her back to their guests.

Aris hadn't been quite sure how the party would turn out, but she did know that the house would be perfect for entertaining. Glancing around the room, she searched the crowd for the few friends she'd invited. Nate and Selah were nowhere in sight so she assumed they'd wandered outside to sit on the deck and enjoy the mild evening air. Deena was in the corner, flirting with the DJ that Luke hired to liven things up after the game ended and the real party began, and Chiki was relaxed on the sofa along with their model friends, Nichelle and Paula, whose striking looks and runway style were generating quite a bit of attention from the single men in their immediate vicinity.

Aris smiled at Chiki who raised her glass of wine in the air and gave her a wink. She nodded and continued to pan the crowd until her eyes found Kim who was standing with Kyle and Troy.

"Kyle is here, standing next to Kim," Aris said to Luke as she pointed to them. "I didn't get a chance to introduce you. Come on."

"I'll be over in a sec, babe. I just heard the doorbell."

Aris nodded and continued toward her friends. She gave Kyle a hug and asked how he managed to slip in without her noticing. Kim said she let him inside, and Aris hugged her animatedly, officially introducing Kim as her best girlfriend in the whole wide world. Just as Kyle was complimenting the house, Luke appeared and shook Kyle's hand in welcome before introducing himself. Aris smiled as they discovered a mutual connection and immediately jumped into their own lively conversation. It was a much different response from Luke's earlier introduction to Troy, which was brief and indifferent at best. As Luke introduced Kyle to another guest a few feet away, Aris tuned into the laughter coming from Troy and Kim.

Troy looked at Aris "I'm going to get Kim another drink. Can I get you anything?"

"Nah. I'm good. Thanks."

Kim's eyes followed Troy. "Yum."

"Troy?" Aris asked in disbelief. "Nooo…"

"Yesss," Kim replied, a sexy smirk appearing on her pretty face. "Hell yes."

"Are you serious?" With a swift shake of her head, Aris grimaced. "Trust me. Troy is like having popcorn kernels stuck in your gums. Like drinking milk the day before its expiration date. Like—"

"Like sexy as shit," Kim added, ogling Troy as he left the kitchen and made his way back over to them. "The way you talk about him, I was expecting a troll…but my, my, *my*." She shifted her eyes to Aris. "I could see myself enjoying him very much."

"Eww."

"Seriously," Kim whispered as Troy handed them both a margarita.

Aris took a generous gulp from her cup and rolled her eyes as Kim laughed and Troy watched them, unsure of what he'd missed while he was gone.

"Just Aris being Aris," Kim shared as she lifted her hand and affectionately played with Aris's hair.

Troy laughed. "No further explanation necessary."

"When did you change your hair anyway?" Kim asked absently. "I'm loving this style on you."

"I don't know…a few weeks ago? Chiki did it and it's pretty easy to keep up. You know I've never been about difficult hair."

"I never imagined you with a wet-wavy look." Kim observed her and smiled. "It's hot."

"You gonna keep it that way?" Troy asked.

Aris shrugged. "Honestly, I prefer it up and out of my face, but I may stick with this for a while."

"You should…though simply wet is my preference."

Troy's eyes swept over her face, his signature smirk in place. "Let me know the next time you need me to hook you up."

Kim's eyes widened and Aris glared at Troy as the room erupted in groans and a few cheers as the opposing team scored a touchdown.

"You need anything, baby?"

Aris jumped as Luke's voice filled her ear. She hadn't noticed that he and Kyle had joined them again. She'd been too focused on Troy and his reckless comment.

Her heart sped up as she looked at Luke. He couldn't have heard a thing, not with the way he was looking at her now, adoration in his eyes. "No, I'm good," she finally said, lifting her hand to show him her cup.

Luke kissed her cheek and excused himself, heading toward Devin who was escorting a few more newly-arrived guests into the family room.

While Troy and Kyle engaged in conversation, Aris absently sipped her drink. She could literally feel Kim's disapproval and wasn't surprised when she was suddenly being pulled away. Kim marched her down the hall to the guest bedroom where she opened the door to find Deena ending a phone call. Kim stormed inside, still pulling Aris along with her.

"Have you lost your damned mind?" Kim snapped, slamming the door before glaring at Aris.

Aris flipped her hand dismissively. "I told you Troy is an ass—"

Kim stomped passed a confused Deena to stand directly in front of Aris. "Please tell me Troy isn't insinuating what I think he's—"

"What? No. Hell no, Kim…are you kidding me?"

"Are *you* kidding *me*?" Kim asked, raising her hands over her head in disbelief. "This man boldly declares how he prefers your hair wet—whatever the hell that's supposed to mean—and says it loud and proud like your man isn't standing less than three feet away...and all you have to say is Troy is an ass?"

Aris turned and moved towards the window.

"Why would he do that, Aris?" Kim prodded. "Please tell me there's nothing going on between you two...but if there is, you better be glad that Luke didn't catch that shit."

"Damn, homie." Deena shook her head, putting the pieces together. "You cheating on Dallas?"

"NO!"

Both women jumped at Aris's tone and watched as she angrily paced the room without looking at either one of them.

"Oooo-kay..." Deena collapsed on the edge of the bed and stared at Aris in complete confusion. "So, you're *not* cheating on Dallas?"

"No, I—" Aris searched for words but fell silent.

"Then what *are* you doing, Aris?"

Aris turned to Kim, heard the warning in her friend's question. It wouldn't be the first time that Kim had called her out on her callousness when it came to the men she dated, but this time Kim's doubt hurt. Because Luke wasn't like the others. After everything Aris had shared with her, Kim had to know that, she had to see that Luke and what she had with him was real for her.

But Kim's eyes said otherwise as she stared at Aris practically expressionless with the exception of the blatant disappointment in her eyes. "Why would you risk it?" When Aris didn't respond right away, Kim turned towards the door to open it. "You're fucking up. Luke is not the one to mess over."

Deena pushed herself off the bed and exited the room as well. When the door closed, Aris ran a hand over her hair and growled a colorful stream of curses as Kim's words lingered in the air.

"You're up."

Aris entered the kitchen to see Nina sitting at the table, drinking a cup of tea. Orange Pekoe from the faint smell of it. It was one of the many individually wrapped bags she swiped from the bar of their Vegas suite weeks ago. Along with the cute little spa products lined up on the bathroom counter. Just the lotion though. She didn't trust using the other ones.

"Yep," Nina replied, circling her hands around the ceramic cup. "Never went back to sleep after Dean and Luke left for a run."

"Oh, I was knocked out." Aris moved toward the refrigerator and opened the door to look inside. "Sorry. If I'd known you were down here, I would have joined you. Made breakfast or something."

"Not at all. I was enjoying the peace. Besides, I'm sure you needed the rest after last night. It was a great party, by the way. I'm glad we were able to make it."

"Thanks." Aris sat at the table, a cup of juice in hand.

Nina smiled at her then took a sip of tea. Aris had only met her one other time almost a year ago. It was the first time Luke had brought her around his family. Nina had smiled at Aris the exact same way then as she was doing now. Like she understood what it felt like to get caught up and make really good mistakes, to wade in a massive pool of doubt and grapple with playing it safe along the wall or letting go to sink or swim in the deep end.

Aris cleared her throat. "You sure I can't get you anything else?"

"I'm fine, truly." Nina looked around. "I absolutely love what you've done with this place."

"Yeah," Aris smiled. "I kinda went overboard, but it's been fun. Guess I was just trying to make it feel more like..."

"Home?"

Aris blinked. Then, she reached up to tuck a strand of hair behind her ear. "Oh, we're just renting. I doubt that we'll stay here for long. I mean, it's home but... I don't really think it's permanent or anything." She smiled nervously and twisted her hands. "But yeah. It works for us. For now."

Nina smiled that same smile again.

Aris hopped up to grab a box of doughnuts.

Returning to the table, she placed the box and some napkins between them. "Have some. Please."

Nina indulged and they sat quietly, enjoying the leftover munchkins from last night. It was an easy, comfortable silence, one that Aris appreciated. She glanced at Nina, whose eyes were focused on a far wall. She was all in her head; Aris could almost see her thinking. It made her grin because it was familiar...and a hint that she clearly had more in common with her boyfriend's cousin's wife than she initially realized. Nina's eyes shifted back to her cup. Lifting it, she took a sip. And a few more after that until she finished her tea. Setting the cup on the table, she stretched. Awakening her body in the manner of a dancer. "Dean scared the shit out of me once too."

Aris blinked again.

"Sorry. I'm not really into small talk." Nina grinned, memories causing her eyes to brighten. "I can sense that maybe you're warring with yourself. Wondering if it makes sense, if you're being foolish, if you're moving too fast. Been there, done that." She laughed a little. "At least you've had some time to figure it out. Dean and I were engaged three weeks after I met him. So whatever you're feeling, I'm pretty sure you can't top what I was going through at that time."

"Three *weeks*?" Aris asked in shock. "I mean, I heard the family talking about it, but I always thought that was, at best, an exaggeration."

"Give or take a day but yep...three weeks. The hell was I thinking, right?" Nina shook her head. "I was a wreck that next month. Second-guessed myself all the way to the altar which was a pretty quick journey because...Dean." She laughed again, the musical sound of it laced with deep affection for her husband. "Once he makes up his mind —"

"He's full speed ahead," Aris finished for her.

Nina smiled again. "Luke too? You'll get used to it."

Aris cut her eyes as they swept Nina from the top of her head to bracelet on her wrist and back up to hold her gaze. "Bullshit."

Nina laughed. "Okay, okay. So maybe you won't...

but you will never be bored." She paused to grab another munchkin, popped it into her mouth and chewed slowly while observing Aris. "Luke loves you. You're safe with him. It's okay to trust that."

The front door opened and closed, followed by loud voices and rowdy laughter. Aris wanted to say more, to ask more, but the time had passed.

Instead, she joined Nina in greeting Luke and Dean as they entered the kitchen with bags full of food.

"I thought y'all went running?" Nina asked.

"We ended up at the gym, shooting around," Dean replied, dropping a kiss on his wife's head.

"I won," Luke added. "No surprise."

Luke was standing behind her and dropped his head to nuzzle her ear before kissing it. The light scent of his cologne activated her senses immediately, causing her to lean into him.

Dean shrugged indifferently at Luke's summation.

Nina grinned at her tight-faced husband. "So this explains breakfast. Good bet. Either way, we all win."

"Nah," Luke replied. "*I* won. Dean paid. We all eat."

"Man, shut yo ass up and get the juice out the fridge," Dean instructed as he eyed Luke with a warning glare. "Make yourself useful or something."

Luke laughed and eased by his older cousin to grab the orange juice from the refrigerator and plastic cups from the cabinet. Once Luke was seated, they joined hands as Dean blessed the table. Then, they ate and talked and joked and laughed until it was time for Nina and Dean to catch their flight back to California.

Later that night, Aris and Luke made love slowly, experiencing their usual bliss together along with something more, something serene, a potent presence of peace that voided all doubts as she reveled in elation and certainty that Luke was hers and she was his.

Nina was right.

Maybe it really was okay to trust that.

Lying in Luke's arms, listening to his soft snores in her ear, Aris snuggled closer. Officially trusting that he loved her and that she was safe with him. That what they had, what they were building together, was real.

As the minutes ticked by, her thoughts shifted to her mess with Troy.

It was a close call.

One that she could never allow to happen again.

Aris closed her eyes. Feeling secure. Feeling happy.

Tomorrow, she would check Troy. Make it clear to him that the stunt he pulled at the party was foul and unwelcomed and not at all the behavior of anyone she would ever call a friend.

Whatever game Troy was playing was one that was of zero interest to her because it was pointless and there would never be a question or competition when it came down to what she really wanted.

Her choice was permanent.

It would always be Luke.

~ *19* ~

"I feel like shit."

Aris smiled. Luke sounded equal parts adorable and pathetic on the other end of her phone line.

"Aww, my poor baby," she cooed. "I'll fix it."

"You're supposed to be here, taking care of me. Now. And rubbing my head. Both of them."

Aris laughed, side-stepping a few of the site crew members to post up behind one of the trailers for some privacy. "That one too, huh?"

"That's the main one."

They talked for several more minutes before Aris noticed Troy standing nearby, appearing to be waiting to end her conversation though it looked more like he was eavesdropping.

Aris pressed her lips together, trying to focus on what Luke was saying to her but she was distracted. Something about the way Troy was invading her space and privacy in that moment irked her, triggering a desire to say the things that needed to be said. She had been tiptoeing around their inevitable confrontation all week. Why? She didn't really know. Perhaps it was because Troy hadn't really done or said anything inappropriate in a while, and it would have felt weird to address her concerns using infractions that occurred days and, in some cases, weeks ago. Saying something about it after so much time had passed could possibly come across as inconsequential, irrelevant. Maybe even slightly petty.

But now…Troy's nosiness served as an impetus.

And the timing couldn't have been better.

"You can't keep doing this," Aris said after ending her call with Luke.

"What?" Troy raised an eyebrow and grinned. "Using my presence to force your distracted ass to get back to work? You've been gone like twenty minutes. Hurry up…I got something to show you."

"You know what I mean, Troy." Aris stepped closer. "We're *friends*. Nothing more. You get that, right?"

Troy's eyes changed but, before he could respond, one of the stylists called out to them and began waving frantically, summoning both back to the set.

Aris glared at Troy, her eyes unwavering.

Troy stared back and nodded his understanding.

It wasn't the most effective conversation but at least she addressed the issue.

In her mind, that's what mattered.

An hour later, they were working side by side on a group of extras. Troy was still himself, full of jokes and sarcasm, not at all bothered by what she told him near the trailers. Actually, they were having a great time much to her relief...until the extras were gone and they were alone again.

"Baby doll...you free next weekend?"

"I am." Aris narrowed her eyes. "And so is Luke."

"Saturday night at seven. My place. Come over."

For a moment, Aris simply stared at Troy. She was about to remind him of their earlier conversation when something else dawned on her. "Wait...I thought you decided the other day to nix the party?"

"Changed my mind. You comin'?"

Troy was staring back at Aris now, waiting for her response. After a moment of silence, he shook his head slowly and grunted. "Dreamboat is welcome too."

Aris remained silent.

Running a hand over his head, Troy observed her discomfort and grinned. "I take it your man has a problem with me and now you do too."

"Yeah, he kinda does," Aris admitted after a brief pause. "Can you really blame him?"

Troy shrugged.

"Seriously, Troy. If we're going to be friends, you gotta stop with all the flirting and the teasing and the questionable comments and shit."

"Okay, baby doll. Whatever you say."

"And that too. Stop calling me baby doll."

"Nah. It suits you." He grinned, reaching up to finger a lock of her hair. "Besides, you know you like it. Tell me you don't."

Rolling her eyes, Aris moved her head from side to side until his hand retreated and he crossed his arms. Ignoring the challenging look in his eyes, she glared at him in defiance. "Don't make me regret being your friend, Troy. I mean it."

"I don't want you to ever regret anything about us."

"I'm serious."

"And I heard you. We're good. Let it go."

"Good. I'm glad we have a clear understanding." Releasing an audible sigh of relief, Aris relaxed her shoulders. "Thank you. And who knows? After a little bit of time, maybe you and Luke could really be cool one day."

Troy hooked his arm around Aris's neck and guided them toward the food truck several yards away. "Let that shit go too."

~ 20 ~

HALLOWEEN

Luke was sitting alone on the sofa, nursing a bottle of beer while watching the silent television as dozens of colorful characters milled about the trendy apartment.

Roughly two hours had passed since he and Aris had arrived dressed as Hawkeye and Black Widow. Luke hadn't particularly wanted to attend the Halloween costume party, but Aris was super excited about it so he decided to humor her by wearing all black and strapping a real bow and some arrows to his back that she "borrowed" from one of her sets. It was the very least he could do since she was always so tolerant and supportive lately of what she never failed to call his "dry ass business dinners."

They arrived about an hour earlier, what some would call fashionably late. Luke sipped his beer and replayed the moment Troy opened the door and ogled

Aris as if she wasn't already spoken for and Luke wasn't standing right next to her. When Troy's eyes shifted to acknowledge Luke, a silent message was passed between them and Troy fell back, literally and figuratively but it was too late because Luke was already pissed. He did his best not to show it—preferably by ramming his fist into Troy's smug-ass face—and kept to himself but, the longer Luke sat and the more time passed, the less interested he was in hiding the fact that he was ready to leave.

It didn't help that the majority of the guests in attendance were strangers except for Kyle, Nate and Selah, who he'd already spent a fair share of time with. While Luke was occupied, Aris got lost in the small crowd, fluttering about, mixing and mingling with her people, which he didn't mind so much until he noticed her across the room with Troy. Luke had been in an animated conversation with Kyle and Nate when he just so happened to turn his head and see Troy taking complete advantage of his too-close promixity to Aris while she talked nonstop, seemingly oblivious to her *friend's* arm around her shoulder.

It had immediately set Luke off.

But he caught himself and played it cool.

Which was why he was sitting alone on the sofa, focusing on the silent television while he struggled to quell the anger that was threatening to take him over at the bullshit playing out right in front of him. The same bullshit that they continued to label a *friendship* when, tonight, they looked a lot less like friends and very much like they were *together*.

Worse than that, others seemed to believe the bullshit

too, despite Aris's spirited introduction of Luke to her friends and colleagues and disclosure of their romantic relationship. Luke had to admit that Aris was on point with proudly letting everyone know who he was and, more importantly, what he meant to her.

That wasn't the problem though.

The real issue was how others seemed to receive it.

Some smiled uncomfortably while a few others' eyes lit up in awkward surprise at Luke's existence, leaving him to feel like he'd been living in the Matrix where Aris was his woman but now the steak was being replaced with a bowl of shit and the fog was lifting to offer a clearer view of what he feared most.

Since then, it had taken everything in Luke to remain calm as Troy took advantage of every possible moment to be in Aris's space, almost parading her around like she was his. Not that Luke could blame Troy for his behavior around Aris; it was the exact same reaction that Luke experienced when he once tried to convince himself that Aris was just his friend.

Been there, done that.

Luke was beyond aware of what Troy was thinking and feeling tonight because, not too long ago, Aris had the very same effect on him. Shit, Luke *was* Troy... which was why the entire scene he witnessed tonight was unmistakable.

What didn't make sense to him was Aris.

She'd appeared oblivious the entire night, playing the happy hostess as expertly as she had a couple of weeks ago at their own house party. Welcoming every guest, giving tours, managing the kitchen and damn near running Troy's apartment as if she knew every square inch…as if it *this* place was her home.

Luke's jaw clenched, surmising that Aris probably spent almost as much time at Troy's as she did at the house she shared with him given how much the trio claimed to be "working"…although Luke now had even more reason to question that pretense after his incredibly enlightening conversation with Selah a short while ago. During a private moment when Kyle and Nate stepped away, Luke and Selah shared a few good-natured jokes about the ridiculous work schedule that Aris, Nate and Troy maintained from week to week, but Luke quickly learned that, unlike Aris, Nate had enough sense to cut his time short and take his ass home leaving Luke to have no choice but to conclude that Aris and Troy were alone together a lot more often than he previously speculated.

Luke took another sip of his warm beer just as a Sasha-Fierce-inspired model strolled over and sat next to him, eagerly seeking his attention by flipping her hair and crossing her legs. Annoyed at his lack of interest, she boldly leaned over so he could appreciate all of her cleavage. "Hi."

Outstanding.

"Hi, I'm Trina," the model purred.

Luke nodded in the woman's direction and took another sip of his beer. There was no reason to speak. *His* woman was across the room, even though Aris had chosen to temporarily forget that fact while playing house with Troy's opportunistic ass.

But Trina refused to let up.

Tired of dwelling on bullshit, Luke finally caved and initiated a meaningless conversation with Trina the

Model and her spectacular cleavage, which only ended up souring his disposition even more. As his responses dwindled from full sentences to one or two terse words, Trina's flirty demeanor quickly turned snide as she followed Luke's gaze to a happy, laughing Aris.

"Oh, I see...so *that's* why you're barely engaged in our conversation." She stood and leaned over Luke, giving him one last peek at her gifts. "Word of advice, handsome. You probably want to leave that one alone. Believe me when I say that Troy nuts up over anyone checking out his girl, so you might want back off."

"Aris Collier," Luke clarified, his eyes darkening as he looked up to catch the barely-veiled jealousy and contempt brewing in the beautiful model's eyes. "She's *Troy's* girl?"

Trina straightened her back and tossed her long, luxurious weave, suddenly bored with their interaction now that she knew there was no chance in hell of getting the results she really wanted from Luke. "Can't say I see what y'all see in her but whatevs."

Luke watched as Trina strutted off toward her next target. He finished his beer and pushed off the wall, his eyes searching for Aris. He found her pouring drinks in the kitchen, practically alone with the exception of a few people standing near her. Although his shoulders relaxed, his jaw was still working. Making his way across the room, Luke watched as Troy materialized and once again eased way too close to Aris, whispering something in her ear to which she rewarded him with cheery giggles and a radiant smile.

"Let's go."

Aris whipped her head around to face Luke with a

dazed yet quizzical expression. He could tell that she was buzzing as she stared back at him in shock, her pouty mouth slightly agape by Luke's tone or maybe by his unwelcomed interruption of her cozy moment with Troy. Either way, her stupefied response pissed him off even more.

Luke shifted his gaze from Aris to Troy. "Don't you have some shit that needs your attention?"

Aris gasped. "Luke, what the—"

He looked pointedly at Aris, his eyes glacial, daring her to finish her statement. She closed her mouth and pressed her lips together in response, turning her back on Troy to glower and swiftly engage Luke in their own private, voiceless conversation.

What the hell is wrong with you? her eyes asked.

Let's go...right now! his returned.

Luke caught Troy's smirk in his peripheral, causing his anger to rise yet another notch to the point where Luke was ready to rearrange dude's face like he'd been imagining himself doing since Troy opened his front door and decided to recklessly cross the line of decency and common sense.

Aris released a frustrated sigh before turning her pleading eyes to Troy. "Can you give us a minute?"

Before Troy could reply to her request, Luke slipped his arm around Aris's waist and pulled her away with him. He ignored the curious glances of random guests and barreled out of Troy's apartment with Aris in tow. Once they reached his car, Luke yanked the passenger-side door open and waited impatiently for Aris to get inside and she did so with much attitude, glaring up at him before slamming the door.

Luke circled the car, jumped in and sped off.

The ride home was tense.

Aris sat stiffly in her seat, her eyes trained on the scenery outside of her window. Music was playing, filling the charged silence between them. Luke didn't trust himself to say anything, not when his words were sure to expose his ire, jealousy and insecurities. The past had already taught him that Aris would definitely not respond well to that approach, so he focused on the lyrics of the music in a desperate attempt to absorb its verbal sentiments of warmth and affection, hoping it would somehow weaken his rage.

Minutes passed before Luke was able to dismiss his emotions and mentally travel back to what he actually saw and heard over the past two hours. Sighing, he glanced at Aris whose face still turned away from him, her body language signaling that he would have to tread lightly.

Luke breathed deeply, regretting how he'd handled the situation, knowing that his behavior had been out of line. He had lost his reason, acting out feelings that he preferred not to have at all. Never in his life did he believe he could lose his shit so quickly and behave so irrationally. During his days with Jessica, rationality ruled. Sure, he recalled feeling and being protective at best but never unhinged, never territorial, never...*this*.

Luke's nostrils flared as a random thought surfaced, generating an amused grunt that rushed up and out of his tense mouth.

He'd never felt this way about Jessica.

Shit, he'd never felt this way about any woman.

Only Aris.

He was beyond in love with her.

"Glad you're over there all amused," she grumbled. "But ain't shit funny 'round here."

Luke laughed a little and pressed the button on the steering wheel to activate cruise control, smiling at the weird surge of serenity that he felt due to his sudden insight and the fact that he was beyond in love with the stubborn ass woman riding shotgun in his car. He shook his head, unable to hold his humor as another amused grunt escaped. It was entirely inappropriate in the midst of what they were going through but, still, he was grateful for the silver lining…

Because now he knew exactly what to say.

Aris was seething.

Not only did Luke totally embarrass her tonight at the party with his caveman antics but now he had the nerve to be laughing about it.

Not trusting herself to look at Luke, Aris kept her eyes focused on the high moon in the dark sky outside of her window…until he began to hum the hook of the love song playing on the radio and she turned to give him a critical once-over. "What the fuck, Luke?"

He glanced her way, appearing contrite. "I'm sorry for that. I was angry—"

"Angry?" she asked, frowning. "About what? Please tell me it's not this Troy shit again…"

He paused for a moment, his eyes back on the road.

Aris cursed under her breath and found the moon

again. "Of course it is."

"I was talking to Trina—"

"Ahh, yes...about *that*." Aris laughed nastily. "Y'all looked pretty cozy over in the corner. I suppose I could have nutted up over that but then I remembered that I was an *adult*..."

Luke glanced at her again. "We were just talking—"

"So were me and Troy," Aris interrupted. "But some of us choose to search for foolishness where none exists and see what we want to see..."

Luke switched lanes and gripped the steering wheel. "It appeared to me that you and Troy were doing more than talking...and I wasn't the only one who saw it."

"Excuse me?" Aris asked, adjusting her body to face him. "Who, pray tell, are these... *people*...cosigning this crap you spittin' right now?"

Luke exhaled to calm himself then shared the details of his conversation with Trina, a model-on-the-prowl that had been circling him most of the night. Aris was already aware of their brief interaction, having noticed it from the second it occurred but she chose to let it ride because Trina was Trina, a thirsty broad who was always looking for her next conquest. It didn't surprise her at all that Luke would quickly see past the model's flashy veneer and be totally turned off by her empty, tiresome talk and shallow advances, which is exactly what happened. Aris's forehead wrinkled, impatient for the point of his uninformative disclosure until Luke repeated the moronic model's falsities and subsequent warning to him "to back off" because of the ridiculous rumor that Aris was "Troy's girl."

"And you believed her?" Aris shrieked.

Luke reduced his speed to exit the highway. "Her words concerned me. Especially the way you and Troy had been carrying on all night. After hearing—"

"So you take the word of a doped up model over what you know to be true?"

"I know what I saw tonight."

"What you *claim*," Aris corrected nastily. "Which was a figment of your fucked up imagination dipped in jealousy and sprinkled with insecurity."

"Moody—"

"*Then*, instead of you coming to talk to me about it, you decide to go full-scale asshole and embarrass me on some suspect info you heard from a broad whose sole agenda was to fuck you." Eyes wide, Aris laughed humorlessly. "But what I still don't quite understand is why not ask *me*, Luke? Better yet, why not just let the shit go...the same way I'm always letting shit go and turning the other cheek when the Evas of the world be tryin' it or when the Renaes block me? Or every single time Jessica drapes her affluent ass over you wherever and whenever she feels prone just to remind us all that bourgeois black Barbie-and-Ken and the Dreamhouse with the elevator ain't never gonna be over."

"What?!" Luke exclaimed in disbelief. "What are—"

"You *know* what I'm talking about!"

Luke gripped the steering wheel again. "Bullshit."

"*Real* shit!" Aris yelled. "I can't count the number of times that I was left to turn a blind eye to the obvious and hear shit about you and Jessica that I didn't want to believe...but did I rush up on your ass in front of your friends and colleagues, demanding that you leave or else like I was your goddamn parole officer?"

Luke didn't respond.

"*Answer me!*"

"Baby..." His voice was weary. "Calm down."

But it was too late. Telling Aris to calm down was like gassing her to go full throttle. Everything she ever wanted to say immediately came tumbling out of her mouth without filter or concern for feelings and, when she was done, the car was deadly quiet the rest of the ride home. Aris was so mad she was shaking, ready to demand that he take her home until it dawned on her that her apartment was no more, that escaping was no longer an option. It was the first time since she moved in with Luke that Aris wished that she hadn't, that she wished she could get away from him.

Luke eased into the garage and Aris's door was open before the wheels stopped rolling. She took off, making her way through the house to their bedroom to strip out of her clothes and step into the shower, all the while flashing back to her previous relationship Ralph Jones, the über-neurotic, green-eyed ex-boyfriend who browbeat her at every turn and never failed to trigger her fight-or-flight response. From the delusions and disputes to the shaming and suffocation, each fretful memory forced its way to the forefront of Aris's mind, triggering her eyes to sting and her throat to tighten until her tears finally fell with the water.

"Moody."

Luke was in the bathroom now, his hand on the door knob. Aris couldn't bear to look at him, so she closed her eyes, hoping that he would just leave her alone.

"Close the door," she choked out. "Please."

Aris waited a moment before opening her eyes.

The door was closed and Luke was gone.

She took her time bathing, the first ten minutes spent standing completely still underneath the scalding hot spray. When the water turned cold, she stepped out and took her time drying off and hanging her towel on the rack before entering the bedroom. Silently, she made her way to the bed and slipped beneath the sheets to focus on ignoring Luke's lingering stares until sleep came to rescue her.

"I'm sorry."

Aris registered the sincerity in Luke's voice before she felt his hand caress her thigh and his lips press against her shoulder, then her face and finally her mouth. The responsiveness of her body to his touch was immediate and inveterate, as it always was. In that moment, her anger retreated as she willingly accepted his muted, passionate apology, allowing herself to get lost in the potent pleasure of connecting with Luke in this way, seemingly the only thing she could ever get right with him.

"Baby," Luke breathed. "I love you so much."

His strokes were slow and strong as he traveled deeper with every thrust.

Her body began to crest. "*Ahhh*...I love you too."

And, just for that moment, all was right with them.

But once her orgasm subsided and the shivers and tingles diminished then disappeared, Aris returned to doubt and distress, staring at the ceiling, wide awake...

Surrounded by Luke's light snores...

Burdened by heavy thoughts...

And consumed with a desperate urge to escape.

~ *21* ~

NOVEMBER

Bag. Jacket. Keys.

Aris departed the house and drove aimlessly until her growling stomach forced her to stop. It was a couple of hours away from noon, so she navigated her way to the nearest restaurant, pancakes on her mind.

"Breakfast for two?"

The teenaged girl at the server stand looked at Aris expectantly. According to the name tag, her name was Violet. It suited her.

"One," Aris replied.

Violet grabbed a menu. "Right this way, ma'am."

The main dining area was almost filled to capacity with lively patrons. Aris was seated at a small table for two near the window, far enough away from the larger party in the vicinity but close enough to still make out their boisterous conversation. As much as she tried to ignore the group, Aris found herself grinning at how extra and inappropriate they were, joking and teasing each other mercilessly. Fortunately for them, they were in the sort of restaurant where its patrons embraced noise and contributed just as much at their own tables.

Tuning them all out, Aris removed her phone from her bag and played a few games until she was able to order a plate of pecan, buttermilk pancakes with extra bacon. When the entree finally arrived at her table, she blessed the food and devoured every last bit of it while scanning her timeline on a popular social media site. There were quite a few pictures posted from Troy's costume party and Aris caught herself smiling as she skimmed the many smiling faces. Scrolling further, she paused at specific post then clicked the photo.

It was a picture of Aris and Troy.

He was standing with his arm around her shoulder, whispering in her ear. Her eyes were closed but her mouth was stretched into a huge smile.

She remembered that exact moment.

He'd been telling her about how he'd caught two of their friends hooking up in his guest bathroom. The visual Troy had painted was so awful that Aris almost choked before laughing long and hard as Troy kept going, taking his colorful commentary way too far.

It had been a funny exchange between two friends.

But the picture made it appear much more intimate.

Aris read Troy's words above the photo.

"Good times with my perfect verse over a tight beat."

Her eyes widened at his public declaration, and she immediately checked to ensure Troy hadn't tagged her. It was a harmless post, but she could only imagine how it would look to Luke if he happened to see it. The very last thing Aris needed today was for Luke to revisit their nonsense from last night.

Noticing the numerous likes for Troy's posted photo, Aris paused only a second before scrolling to read the comments, most of which were harmless as well... except for a few trolls who eagerly and foolishly chose to jump to crazy conclusions about the nature of their relationship as a result of their proximity to each other and overall body language in the photograph.

Aris stared at the photo again.

"Would you like some more water?"

Pressing the home button to clear the image from her phone, Aris looked up and smiled at the server. "No, umm...thank you. Can I get the check, please?"

"Certainly." The woman smiled as she removed a printed ticket from the bill folder in her apron and placed it face down on the table. "Enjoy your day."

"Thanks. You too."

Snatching the ticket from the table, Aris stood and snaked her way out of the dining room toward the retail area. Minutes later, she was inside of her car with the engine running, in no rush to go anywhere.

A chime sounded from her bag.

Removing her phone, she checked the notifications.

More likes and comments on Troy's picture.

Aris logged off, put the car in drive and sped away.

Her next stop was the mall...of all places. Aris was in no mood to shop, but she found a parking space near the entrance of one of her favorite department stores, convincing her that the upscale center was clearly where she was supposed to be.

Because she definitely wasn't ready to go home.

With no particular destination in mind, Aris strolled the mall and literally window shopped.

While still thinking about Luke.

He was still in bed when she'd left the house earlier although she was certain he wasn't completely asleep. She didn't even bother to check, not wanting to deal with him just yet after their argument last night.

"Errands."

One word. That's all she'd said to him on her way out of the bedroom and he didn't even budge or offer a response to her lame ass excuse, which was more than fine…because she hadn't wanted one.

But now, hours later, she did.

She wanted to hear his voice. She wanted to erase everything that happened at the party last night and permanently dissolve the tension between them and get back to being in love.

Abruptly stopping in her tracks, Aris whirled around and rushed back to the lingerie store at the other end of the mall. By the time she walked through the entrance, her mind was spinning with possibilities.

Level up.

Smiling, she searched the sale and clearance racks, hoping to find the perfect ensemble that screamed "I'm sorry" and "fuck me" at the same damn time. After exhausting the discount areas, Aris reluctantly moved to the new arrivals near the front of the store and along the walls. Scanning the merchandise, her eyes were immediately drawn to a super sexy corset. It was the right look but pain was not a part of her plan, so she redirected her attention to the soft material of a pretty, plunge teddy. She reached out to finger the lace and tiny bows when a voice interrupted.

"That's made for you," the man said.

Aris cringed.

What the hell is he doing here? Aris thought as she turned to face Ralph Jones. After a lengthy pause, she decided to voice her exact thoughts. "Ralph. What are you doing here?"

He smiled. It was familiar and annoying all at once. "Shopping."

Aris crossed her arms. "What are you doing *here*...in Atlanta?"

"I'm in town for a few days," he replied. "Business."

As far as Aris knew, Ralph still lived in Dallas. She hadn't seen him since the night he and Luke had a dick measuring contest in the middle of her living room. Screening him from head to toe now, Aris admitted to herself that Ralph looked the same — good — but she was happy to acknowledge that she still felt absolutely nothing for him.

Aris crossed her arms, already bored. "Yet, you're in the middle of a lingerie store."

"I have a friend who lives in Smyrna," Ralph replied with a small smile. "But had I known there would be even the slightest chance of me running into you..."

Aris frowned. "I have a man."

To Ralph's credit, he didn't react to her update. So unlike him. "Lucky man. Serious?"

"Permanent."

Ralph laughed hard at that, causing Aris to wrinkle her nose at what she could only assume was source of his amusement — the reality about her.

The ugly truth.

"Permanent has never been you, love." Ralph looked at Aris, the statement he made and the regret in his eyes absolute confirmations that her assumption was correct. "Does your new man know that yet?"

She lifted her chin and presented her best resting bitch face. "Take care of yourself, Ralph."

Leaving the teddy behind, Aris strutted out of the store and fought the shame that was beginning to cover her like a clock. That Ralph would say the very thing that she had been trying to force back into the corner of her mind since her fight with Luke last night was certainly not a coincidence.

Permanent has never been you…

Does your new man know that yet?

Aris ran a hand through her hair and picked up her pace. Soon, she was driving away from the mall then looping I-285 until she was again passing the same mall where Ralph's words sent her on a random drive to outrun her troublesome thoughts.

Looping definitely wasn't working.

Because she needed to actually *work*.

Without pause, Aris grabbed her phone and dialed Nate's number.

"Hey," he answered.

"Hey…I was thinking we could put in some work today." May as well cut to the chase. "You free?"

"Nah," he replied quickly with a smile in his voice. "Selah's over here whupping my ass in Wii Tennis. I must now spend the afternoon redeeming myself."

"Whupping…his…ass! Yeeeaaaahhhh!"

Aris laughed at Selah's cosign in the background.

"She got you playing video games? Impressive."

"I know, right?" Nate replied, sounding all kinds of happy. "What you won't do..."

"You do for love," Aris finished for him. "If that ain't the truth..." She paused. "You talked to Troy today?"

"Yeah, earlier. He hit me up about work too."

"Ahh, great minds think alike. I'll call him." She made an illegal U-turn and sped in the direction of Troy's apartment. "Don't get your ass beat too bad, Nate...know your limits."

"Ha. Ha. Later."

She smiled. "Later, love birds."

Aris drove about five miles before Ralph's words came back to her mind again. Deep in thought, her right foot slipped and her car steadily slowed until a car horn blared and she pressed the gas pedal.

"All right," she mumbled, switching lanes. "Relax."

Aris passed the exit to Troy's apartment with a new destination in mind.

Home.

When she entered the house, Luke was on the sofa in the family room with an empty container of what she assumed were hot wings sitting on the coffee table in front of him.

"I ordered you some too," he said without even looking at her. "Left it in the oven. Wasn't sure if you ate while you were...wherever you were."

Aris moved through the kitchen and into the family room to stand next to the sofa he was sitting on. Her intention had been to sit but that was before his sarcastic ass comment pissed her completely off. "I'm not hungry."

"So you ate?"

"No," she replied. "I didn't eat."

"So what did you do?"

Aris closed her eyes and took a deep breath.

So what did you do?

Luke spoke those words in a way that suggested that she was off doing something that she wasn't supposed to be doing...like he didn't believe that she'd simply gone to the mall and went inside lingerie store to buy something for his suspicious ass in an attempt to make up and resolve this tension between them...like it was too far-fetched to believe that she'd been thinking of him the entire time she'd been away...

Her indignation slipped as a crystal clear image of Ralph's assured expression appeared in her mind.

Permanent has never been you...

Does your new man know that yet?

"I went to the mall."

Luke finally looked at her. "Did you buy anything?"

"No."

His eyes traveled back to the sitcom he'd been watching before she arrived and they didn't speak again until the next commercial.

"What else did you do?"

"Drove around."

"Drove around?"

"Yeah." Aris crossed her arms. "Problem?"

Luke observed her stance. "I'm not trying to fight with you, baby. I was just curious how you spent your morning away from me because I missed you."

The ice cracked and her heart sped up.

He could always do that.

Melt her with a word, a look, a touch, a smile.

"I missed you too."

Aris considered telling Luke about her run-in with Ralph at the mall, but she was done with this tension pulling them apart. Telling Luke about Ralph would only jump-start their bickering, which seemed to, at least for now, be over.

Ralph wasn't that serious.

Pushing her ex's words to the darkest corner of her mind, Aris eased onto the sofa and into Luke's arms, resting her head on his shoulder.

They remained that way until Aris's phone buzzed.

When she didn't answer it, Luke asked her why.

She said she didn't need to.

When he asked her why again, she sat up to face him and quickly registered the doubt and disappointment she saw in his eyes.

That pissed her off again.

"Don't do this."

"What am I doing?" he asked, his eyes blank.

She held his gaze. "Trying to control me."

He didn't hide his surprise. "What?"

"Your controlling behavior has to stop."

Luke frowned, appearing more confused than angry. He searched her eyes. "Where is this coming from?"

When Aris simply stared at him, Luke ran a hand down his face and released a weary breath.

"I'm not trying to control you, Moody—"

"Then, what's with the interrogation?"

Luke looked down at his hands and clasped them together, his frustration beginning to surface. "So me asking you what you've been up to for the afternoon and why you suddenly don't need to answer your phone is wrong...but you hopping your ass up this morning, attitude and all, no more than one word spoken to me before you left and then not hearing from you for hours is right?"

"I had my phone. You could have reached out."

"Why? So you can ignore my call too?"

Aris narrowed her eyes but remained quiet.

"And now you're actually sitting here telling me to stop *interrogating* you...like I don't have the right to know where my damn girlfriend is and what she's doing when she's not with me."

"That's what I'm talking about," Aris said, her hands in fists. "*That*. The way you always suggest that when I'm away from you, I'm doing something wrong."

"That's not what I meant—"

"That's *exactly* what you meant." Aris stood to her feet and looked down at Luke. "I went through this shit before with Ralph...I'm not doing this again!"

Luke's head snapped up at the mention of Ralph's name. "Where the hell did that come from?"

"I'm making a point—"

"No, what you did was bring him up...out of nowhere." Luke's voice was dangerously quiet. "You haven't so much as mentioned your life in Dallas beyond Kim and suddenly Ralph is now a part of our discussion. The question is...why?"

"No." Aris clenched her teeth, her eyes flashing. "The real question is why should I endure another insecure ass man in my life? Why should I be made to feel like I'm the one always doing something wrong?"

Luke looked at her like she was speaking Mandarin.

"What the hell are you even talking about right now?"

"I'm talking about you behaving just like Ralph—

"Make that the last time that you ever compare me to that man...or any other for that matter. Understood?"

Luke's eyes held warning, his face a mask of anger.

"Fine." She tossed her head and crossed her arms. "But it doesn't change the fact you are being insecure, controlling, suffocating—"

"So I'm suffocating you now?" Luke ran a hand over his head in disbelief and laughed. It was a sarcastic sound, meant to goad her.

It worked.

"You're trying to force me to be her," Aris explained. "...and I'm not."

Luke frowned. "Who?"

"Jessica."

"Get the fuck outta here..." His eyes jumped around the room as he spread his arms out beside him, palms up. "And where the fuck did *that* come from?"

"I am *not* Jessica." Aris's voice was shaky, and she looked away, running both hands roughly through her hair to calm herself before she spoke again. "This is *me*. I'm not perfect, but this is what you get. If that's suddenly no longer good enough for the great Luke Donovan, then say that and go back to your Barbie Doll. I'm sure she'd be happy to tolerate this type of shit from you again and welcome you back with open arms. Ain't like she hasn't been waiting around for it."

"Moody." Luke made a tent over the bridge of his nose with his fingers. His tone was calm, measured... but she could tell he was still boiling underneath the surface. He stood and moved toward her until they were toe-to-toe, his eyes boring into hers. "I don't know how we got here, but let me be clear. I apologize if you feel like I'm controlling you. That is not and never has been my intention. I love you—everything about you. If you don't know this by now, then I've obviously done something wrong—"

"Damn right, you've done something wrong," Aris said, her voice finally breaking. "Jessica can be all over you and I gotta shut the fuck up about it, but then you turn around and accuse me every five minutes of some foul shit." She curled her lip, shaking her head. "Looks to me like you're projecting. So...what did *you* do?"

"You're not serious," Luke replied, looking at her as if she'd lost her mind. "Moody, what the hell is all this really about?"

Instead of responding with the truth, Aris turned away and backtracked to the kitchen, snatching the extra container of hot wings from the oven on her way to yank the door to the garage wide open and slam it on her way out.

Aris fully expected Luke to text or call her...

Before she revved the engine to her car.

Before she left the subdivision.

Before she drove to Troy's place.

But he didn't.

Aris sat in her idling car for ten minutes.

Waiting for Troy to get home.

Sure, she had a key to let herself in but she wasn't

quite sure she really wanted to do that because Luke had finally called — three times actually, back-to-back — and she was fighting her urge to go home and fight him again.

She was so tired of fighting.

She needed a break.

Exhausted by their argument and Luke's controlling behavior overall, Aris eventually silenced her phone and emerged from her car just as Troy pulled into the parking space next to her.

"How long have you been waiting out here?" he asked after activating his car alarm. "Lost your key?"

"I just got here," Aris lied, following him up to his apartment. "Key is in my bag."

Troy unlocked and opened the door, extending his arm to allow Aris to enter first. "What's up, baby doll? I didn't expect to hear from you today, then you ask to stop by and now you're being weird."

"I'm always weird."

Troy grinned. "True. But your eyes are sad. Tell me what's wrong."

"Nothing you can fix."

"Try me."

Aris looked into his eyes...and ignored what she thought she saw. "Can we work?"

"Yes. We always work." Troy took a bold step closer before hesitating, carefully observing Aris before his eyes suddenly narrowed in understanding of what she truly meant. "You got something specific in mind?"

"No. I didn't plan this." She sighed and collapsed onto the sofa. "Sorry for barging in. I just needed to get away for a minute."

"Don't ever apologize for needing me."

"I need to work," she clarified.

"That too."

"Then let's get to it."

"No music?" Troy asked.

Aris forced a little smile. "Always music."

A few minutes later, the sounds of contemporary jazz filled the air and set a relaxed setting as Aris began working on one of Troy's mannequin heads. They debated her approach, Troy pushing Aris to dig deeper for a more original idea but she soon became frustrated by his incessant questioning and dropped her head in her hands, abandoning her efforts altogether.

"What's with you today?"

Lots of sighs was her reply.

"Relax." Rising from the sofa, Troy went to grab some materials, tools and a chair from his dining room table and brought them back to where Aris was working. He positioned the chair and sat facing her. "Forget the mannequin. For now, just paint. On me."

A smile played at Aris's lips.

"Don't act like you haven't ever used me before."

She laughed. "Okay. Twenty-minute sprints?"

"Yeah, I'll clock it." Troy set the timer on his phone.

"Rules?"

"No rules, baby doll. Just work."

Her eyes lit up. "Okay."

"Burn." Troy watched as she quickly arranged her tools. "Latex. Lube. Cotton. Alcohol. Tissue paper. Ground coffee." He waited again as she rushed around his apartment to collect the materials.

"Ready?" he asked when she returned.

Nodding, she bounced around in excitement.

"Forearm." He lifted the sleeve of his shirt. "Go."

Aris worked frantically for the next fifteen minutes and when Troy's phone beeped that her time was up, she stepped back and listened eagerly to Troy's in-depth critique.

"Next?" she asked after the debrief was done.

"Cut," Troy replied. "Flat Mold. Alcohol. Q-tips."

He added a few more items as Aris gathered them quickly and arranged them on the table along with her tools. After a final check, she nodded her readiness.

"Throat." Troy set the timer. "Go."

While creating an impressive slit throat, Aris sang and bounced around. She joked and laughed with Troy as a welcomed sense of contentment from her sprints replaced the tension she arrived with over an hour ago.

"Feeling better?" Troy asked.

Aris looked up and winked, then dipped her head to continue working and singing until the phone beeped.

Only this time, it wasn't Troy's timer.

He raised a brow. "You need to answer that?"

"Nope. I'm working."

Aris stopped singing as she finished the last touches to Troy's neck. Stepping back, she grabbed and mirror and handed it to him.

"The color is on point." Troy turned his head to get a better angle. "Blending...detail...yeah. Nice work."

Aris nodded. Her forced smile was back.

Troy tweaked her nose. "You want to tell me what's wrong now?"

"I'm straight. Go clean yourself up."

Troy stared pointedly at Aris before he left to do as

she asked. She took advantage of that alone time to think and clean up the mess they'd made. When Troy returned to the living room, she was sitting on the sofa with a glass of wine in her hand, staring at the blank television screen.

"It's more entertaining if you turn it on."

"Ha...ha..." She took a long sip. "Ha."

He joined her on the sofa and guided her head to rest against his shoulder. "Who erased the smile I worked so hard to put on your face?"

She took another sip of wine. "How's Darby doing?"

"She's good. Probably doing lunch and hanging out with her girlfriends. Shopping sprees or some shit."

"Why wasn't she at your Halloween party?"

"Because it wasn't that serious."

Aris lifted her head and faced him. "For real. Why?"

"Because I didn't tell her about it."

Aris bit her lip, still unsatisfied with his answer to her question, still wanting to ask why again...but it never came out.

Because Troy kissed her.

The first one was tentative. Exploratory. Aris was frozen, her heart beating rapidly as he pressed his lips against hers again, this time with urgency. She felt his hands move into her hair, cupping her face as if he was afraid she would slip away. He said her name in a whisper, an almost desperate edge lacing his voice.

She was still frozen.

Pulling away, Troy ran the pad of his thumb over her bottom lip and she shuddered involuntarily at the sensation, a positive response that motivated him to taste her lips again and tease and suck and tease again, every kiss urging her to finally let the inevitable happen between them.

It felt good. More than good, it felt great…

But it didn't feel *right*.

Aris turned her head and stood abruptly to cross the room, to put distance between them, to stop what could happen between them, what she had no doubt *would* happen between them if they were to ever give themselves a real chance.

Their chemistry was palpable.

But it didn't make it right.

She took a deep breath. "This was a mistake."

"Was it?"

Turning around, Aris pressed her lips together. She was visibly rattled and at a loss for what came next.

"Talk to me."

She remained silent.

"You won't tell me what's going on, but obviously it's serious enough for you to ignore your phone. You won't tell me why you were sad before you got here but, for the past hour, I made you smile." Troy held her gaze until she dropped her eyes. "Of all the places you could've gone, you chose to come to me."

Still unable to respond, Aris rushed over to her bag and tossed her phone inside. When she reached for her jacket, Troy reached for her hand but she snatched it back and moved back to the other side of the room. The sound of her heartbeat was in her ears, her breaths escaping in short, erratic bursts. She forced a shaky hand through her hair and shut her eyes.

"There's a reason for that," Troy said in a low voice. "There's a reason for all of this."

"Stop." Aris finally looked at him, her eyes pleading. "Stop talking."

"We've been dancing around this since we met."

"There is no *this*," Aris said in a clipped voice. "What just happened was a terrible mistake."

"It wasn't a mistake."

"Shut. Up."

Troy tried to come closer and Aris dodged his advances, putting more distance between them until they squared off from opposite ends of the coffee table.

"I'm in love with you, Aris. You know that."

"Please. Stop. Talking."

Silence covered them as they stared at each other.

"I'm not asking you for anything," Troy said, his eyes never wavering. "I'm not trying to force anything. Nothing about us has ever been forced, so I'm sorry if it felt that way when I kissed you. I wanted to, I *needed* to kiss you...but I understand why you weren't ready to kiss me."

"Please. Don't. Do. This."

"I can't help it. Everything about you is beautiful to me. I see how you take risks, how you think and make sense of everything. The way you sing at the top of your lungs when you're happy and your pitiful attempts at dancing. How you wrestle with doubt, yet you never stop trying. Your stubborn streak, your desire to fly and that sparkle in your eyes. I know exactly who you are, Aris Collier. I get you, I want you, I need you...baby doll, you are *it* for me."

"And Luke is it for *me*."

There was a long pause as Aris glared at Troy in defiance but his eyes remained hopeful, daring her to acknowledge what they already knew.

"Fine," Troy conceded. "But at least admit it."

Aris took off. "I'm out of here."

"It's not so unusual you know," Troy said, his words stopping her from rushing out of his front door. Her back was to him and, though she wanted to bolt, she couldn't help but listen. "It makes sense that there's something between us."

"There's nothing between us. Not even friendship." She swung around and scowled. "Not anymore."

"I get that you're angry," Troy said carefully. "I'm not exactly thrilled either, Aris. Contrary to what you may be thinking about me right now, I didn't set out to want another man's woman. You think I don't know that this is wrong? You think I actually want to feel this way about you? Well, I don't...but I don't lie to myself either. There's something between us. Admit it."

Aris stood completely still, warring with herself.

"Just...just give me something. Tell me...I just need to hear you say it. Just once and...fuck." Troy ran both hands over his head in frustration. "You got me rambling. I can't believe I'm even doing this shit—"

"I feel something. For you."

Troy dropped his hands and stared at Aris, hope brimming in his eyes. "Aris—"

"Let me finish." She bit her lip, unsure of her next words. "I don't want to feel whatever it is I feel for you and I suppose I've been ignoring it. Ignoring you. Because it's not right."

"It's not right, but it's real."

Absorbing his words, Aris stared at Troy, long and hard, realizing that Luke was right about him. Worse than that, Luke and Ralph were right about her.

Had she done this?

Had she once again let this happen under the guise of "friendship"...the same way she'd done with Luke, Marcel, Ralph, Shane, David...

Was she doing it again now? With Troy?

Permanent has never been you...

Aris looked away, covering her mouth with a shaky hand as the truth hit her with the force of a hurricane.

That was exactly what she had done.

She couldn't help herself.

It was in her nature.

All that shit she was talking during her arguments with Luke last night and again today were simply a cover, her complete denial about what she had been doing with Troy and what she was doing right now.

Luke was right.

He had to protect their relationship at all costs.

And though Troy had been the suspect...

Aris was the real culprit.

And now she'd just risked losing the one person who really loved her.

"It's selfish of me, really," Aris clarified. "I'm just being weak and...and I guess maybe I've caused all of this. You're right. There's a reason for all of this, and it's me. We were friends and I allowed this to happen. I have been wrong in our dealings with each other. I have pretended not to know that there is something going on between us, but I have to own that now. And in doing so, I have a choice to make. And I choose Luke. And in choosing him, I have to let this...our friendship...or whatever it is between us...I have to let it go." She dropped her head and pressed her lips together, once again searching for the right words to do what she should have done from the moment their relationship was compromised. "I don't know what I really feel for you, Troy. I never once explored it, and I don't intend to...because I choose Luke." Lifting her head and held his gaze so there would be no further misunderstandings. "From this point on, we are only colleagues. We can no longer be friends."

Troy immediately launched into a heartfelt response in an attempt to reverse her decision but Aris simply ignored him and gathered her things on her way, stopping only to leave the key he gave her on the coffee table. Without looking back, she put even more distance between them and opened the front door.

Troy called her name, wanting her to stay.

She didn't respond and walked out of his apartment for the very last time.

~ 22 ~

"It is done."

Aris paused dramatically and waited.

"Ooo-kay?" Kim replied. "Mind saying hello first and then telling me what the hell we're talking about?"

"Troy," Aris clarified. "He has been firmly colleague-zoned as of oh-six-hundred-hours. Mission complete."

"By whom?"

"Me. Who else?"

"Well, well," Kim said. "About damn time. I take it Mr. Troy finally took a bit too much of your rope and hung himself with it?"

"Resorting to the old I-told-you-so? Really, Kim?" Aris sucked her teeth. "That's so beneath you."

"Not at all. I'm petty and I'm proud."

"Whatever. Point is...it's done."

"What do you mean...done?"

Aris frowned. "What I just said."

"Your definition of done has always been sort of questionable, Aris, not to mention the fact that Troy's colleague-zone is still pretty suspect in my mind, so please...humor me."

"There's nothing funny."

"Fine, don't," Kim replied. "But you could at least tell me what happened to finally make you come to your senses."

"Troy kissed me."

"What?!"

Aris pulled the phone from her ear as Kim continued to react to old news. Once the yelling stopped, she tuned back in to more of Kim's I-told-you-so's. Rolling her eyes, Aris cut Kim off and told her the rest of the story and how she made it clear to Troy in no uncertain terms that they could no longer be friends.

"Good for you," Kim said, pride in her voice. "It takes two and it was very mature of you to admit the part you played in all of this too. I just wish you'd done that weeks ago, but never mind that. What matters is you did what needed to be done and all that drama is finally over."

"Yep."

"Are you okay?"

"I'm fine," Aris replied, a little too quickly.

"Seriously," Kim insisted, her voice full of concern. "It's okay if you're not. Despite Troy's inappropriate remarks and boundary issues, I get that he was still your creative buddy. It sucks that you'll lose that, but it's the right thing to do. You know that, right?"

"Yep."

"You're not listening."

"I am listening. I'm fine with it."

Kim released a weary sigh. "You're not, but you will be. Especially when you tell Luke about it."

"I will do no such thing."

"Pardon?" Kim asked, her Texas twang surfacing.

"Why add more fuel to a dying fire? What happened between me and Troy was a one-time—"

"Fling," Kim inserted, sarcastically.

"*Thing*," Aris snapped. "Shut ya face."

"Mmhmm…"

"For real…what happened between me and Troy was an unfortunate mistake. And now it's done. Never to ever—*ever, ever*—happen again. Why tell Luke now and add more drama when the situation has already been resolved?"

"Oh, Aris—"

"Oh, shut it!" Aris spat. "To the grave, wench."

"Fine." Kim sighed again in defeat. "To the grave."

"Honey…I'm hooome!"

Aris floated through the door into the kitchen feeling light and burden-free. For the past few days, her focus had been on simply beginning again. Luke had been out of town for a few days so, while he was away, Aris had holed up in the house and cut herself off from the world. The only calls she answered were from Luke, Kim, Tony and Celeste…but most of her talk time was with Luke.

Occasionally, there were moments when she felt like

picking up the phone and calling Troy to brainstorm and talk shop, but she would dial Nate instead.

But it wasn't like talking to Troy.

The change in their status really helped her to recognize how much she'd leaned on Troy in the past and how much she sought him when she freaked and spazzed and pretty much couldn't handle herself. He'd been a genuine confidant who gave her the best advice and was the perfect audience. It was a sobering truth that never failed to leave Aris feeling both empty from her loss and remorseful that it had undermined her relationship with Luke.

But she had plans to fix the latter.

Aris set the take-out bags on the kitchen counter and removed the food containers. She called out to Luke, telling him to come eat, then turned to see him standing right behind her with tired eyes and a pleased grin on his face. Rising to her toes, she sprinkled kisses along his jaw before brushing her lips across his. Her intent had been to give him a quick peck but his arm snaked around her waist and pulled her closer to him as his tongue danced with hers.

"I missed you."

"I missed you too." After one last kiss, Aris returned to food handling. "You hungry? I got your favorite."

"I am. Thank you, baby."

Luke helped Aris with the food, and they bypassed the table to stretch out on the sofa. The television never came on as their conversation entertained them for the better part of an hour, long after their food was eaten. It was an easy hour of silly stories and light-hearted laughter, of two unlikely friends who became lovers and created their own language then got drunk enough to schedule a drive-thru wedding and sobered up to share space and live happily ever after.

It was perfect.

Aris poured what was left of a bottle of wine into her glass. Her heart was full, and she knew without a doubt that she was where she was meant to be. That Luke would always be the best part of her day.

The best part of her life.

"I really missed you."

Luke let his eyes sweep Aris's face and body and he blessed her with a lazy, sexy smile. "I love that you miss me, and I hate it at the same time. I know this travel is hell. It'll get better, Moody, I promise."

"I didn't say that to start a guilt trip—"

"I know," Luke clarified, caressing her leg. "I just mean that I know how hard all this traveling has been on us both. I hate being away from you, especially when you need me. I just need you to hang in there with me—when it gets rough, when you feel like it's not worth it or when I'm not worth it, when it's easier to do something easier—don't forget what we have. Because when I'm gone, I still need *this*." He gestured his hand between them, the movements meant to illustrate their connection. "I need you to still be here with me. Because I'm always with you."

Aris let his words hang in the air as she thought about her conversation with Kim, but then she smiled as something else that suddenly surfaced in her mind.

I'm not alone anymore.

It was the one thought that always made her heart flutter, the one that still caught her off guard and forced a goofy grin to form on her lips because, for the first time in her life, she had someone in her corner. A voice of reason and endearment, of inspiration and motivation. A voice other than her own. Someone with whom she could genuinely share everything. Random things. Silly things. Serious things. Useless things. To Aris, Luke had always been like a real-life diary that she filled with every moment of her life.

When had that happened?

She couldn't recall. Perhaps it was an accidental occurrence on an arbitrary day or maybe she and Luke had been sitting around and he simply asked her what was on her mind and, instead of her routine "nothing" response, maybe she saw something different in his eyes or heard something more in his voice that triggered her to spill her guts, then spill them again later that same night and the night after that...because it felt like she should...and because he really listened.

Her heart dropped at another realization.

When had that *changed*?

Her smile faltered a bit as the answer loomed like a dark cloud over their heads, the proverbial elephant in the shadiest corner of their family room.

Staring at Luke now, Aris felt a little bit like she imagined she must have felt on that arbitrary day, a feeling of transparency, like she should open her mouth and spill her guts. Spill Troy.

But she didn't.

Because, for the first time, Aris wasn't certain if she should or if Luke would stick around to really listen.

To the grave.

Those three words bounced around in her mind until

she settled on sharing another truth, a better truth. One that would mend and not break them, one that would officially displace and bury the funky elephant that wasn't supposed to be lurking in the corner, stinking up their surroundings and clogging up her conscious.

A truth she once heard and received herself.

"I know and so will I," Aris finally replied, the words flowing easily from her mouth, from her heart, from her spirit. "I'll always be here with you and wherever you are when you're not with me. I'd do that and whatever else you need me to do so that you can feel safe, comfortable and secure."

Luke grinned, recognizing her words. "Why?"

"Because you're worth it." Aris leaned forward and kissed him. "And because, for the first time in my life, I'm not alone anymore. And I never once cared about that until I met you...which makes me want to do and be whatever you need whenever you need it so I can flip whatever negative mood that may be stressing you because it's my job to make you smile."

Grinning, Luke narrowed his eyes. "Look at you... trying to be me."

"Hell nah," she replied, wrinkling her nose as she moved closer to him and shifted to align her body with his. "I'm just trying to be the best me for you."

He nodded. "I like that."

She stole another kiss. "I thought you would."

~ 23 ~

Luke shifted the gear into park and cut the engine. He let the window down halfway and reclined a little, waiting on Aris to come out of the building after ending her work day which should be in about fifteen minutes because of his early arrival. He'd left the office about two hours ago, way too much on his mind to work, all of it involving Aris...more specifically, their relationship.

The past couple of months had been nonstop. Luke thought back to the car ride from Sunday dinner all those weeks ago. Maybe Aris had been right. Perhaps it really had been too soon to move in together. It was no question that they loved each other enough, but maybe they weren't ready for this next step.

Maybe he had been wrong.

Just as that thought occurred to him, it was replaced with memories of the day he and Aris moved into the house. So much laughter. So much hope.

Where had all that gone?

It was easy to see the stress that Aris was under. She worked too damned much, too damned hard, just as he did. Maybe it was time to press pause.

Maybe it could start with him.

For weeks, he'd been anxious to catch a plane for something other than business, to take a break from the routine. They needed another trip, another Vegas. Some time to block everyone and everything else out. Their schedules would probably interfere, but at this point, even a staycation would be better than nothing.

Luke considered reserving a fancy room somewhere nearby, possibly the The Ritz-Carlton or The Georgian Terrace. They could stay hidden away in bed, ordering room service and enjoying each other.

Running a hand over his mouth, Luke glanced at the clock on his dashboard and blinked at how quickly the time had passed. He'd been sitting in the car for twenty minutes…where was Aris?

His first thought was to text her but his hand reached for the door release instead. After securing the alarm on his car, he moved toward the building's entrance. He had no idea where to find her, so he pulled out his phone, ready to call, but stopped at the bottom of the concrete stairs when he noticed Troy exit the building and descend the stairs toward him. Luke nodded at him in greeting, intending to pass without a word.

Troy cleared the bottom step and stood facing Luke with his hands in his pockets. "Aris asked me to tell you that she's occupied for the moment."

Luke's eyes shifted and his right hand flexed at his

side. Troy's satisfied smirk begged to be adjusted but, after an extended pause, Luke simply turned away and reached for his phone to call Aris.

"I'll send her out when we're done."

Luke swung around. "Fuck you say?"

Troy kept his stance and offered no words.

"Make no mistake…" Luke moved in an instant, stopping only when he and Troy were toe-to-toe, eye-to-eye. "I tolerate you, bruh. To keep the peace. If you don't want real problems, I suggest you watch your words around me and keep it professional with her at all times…ya feel me?"

Troy shrugged dismissively, riling Luke even more. After a few tense moments, Troy's smirk was back. "Too late for that…on both counts."

In the blink of an eye, Troy was on the ground.

His smirk was still in place as he stood to his feet and swiped the pad of his thumb over his busted lip.

In the distance, they heard a door slam closed.

A security guard stood at attention, surveying the area before his gaze locked on them. Troy pivoted, climbed the stairs and addressed the officer by name. They exchanged words and Troy slapped a hand on the man's back. In that same moment, Aris exited the building and waved to Troy and the officer. She immediately reacted to Troy's injury, and Luke could hear her demanding to know what happened to him before she searched her bag and removed what appeared to be a tissue.

Luke's jaw clenched.

After shaking her head and giving Troy a hug, Aris descended the stairs. She looked from left to right, searching the parking lot.

When she spotted Luke, she smiled.

Rushing over, Aris stopped in front of Luke to give him a hug as well but he turned and headed for the car. The noise from the items in her bag and backpack were the only indications that she was following him.

Easing into the car, he waited for her to get inside before he started the ignition and sped out of the parking lot.

"Hey." Aris said, giving Luke a tentative smile. "I'm sorry I was late coming out. I ran into Troy and the strangest thing happened...he said that he tripped and busted his lip." She shook her head. "Anyway, I was running behind because I had to finish up a mold and it took a lot longer than I expected." Aris waited for Luke's response but there was nothing but silence. "It couldn't be helped... I'm really sorry. Are we late for something? Why are you driving so fast?"

Eyes on the road, he didn't respond.

"Guess you're in a place," she mumbled to herself but made sure it was loud enough for him to hear her. "Fine. I'll wait."

Waiting must have gotten old for her really fast because less than two minutes later Aris started a one-sided conversation about everything except what Luke needed to know. Troy's words were still fucking with him, his violently churning gut signaling that Troy's reckless ass comment might actually be true.

"Just tell me why."

Aris glanced at Luke, unable to find the right words to answer his question. They were standing in their bedroom, and Luke finally came out of his place to tell her the real reason why Troy's lip was busted. She'd asked Troy a few times while she dug in her bag to find him a tissue because she hadn't really believed that he tripped and fell. He brushed her off each time, tossing her his usual smirk.

Now she knew why.

"Luke," Aris began but then she fell silent.

"I basically told that man to keep his hands off you to which he replied and I quote...too late for that." Luke pinned her with a furious gaze. "Tell me why he said that. Tell me why you did whatever it is that you did to make him say that."

"Luke, nothing happened."

"Do not lie to me."

"I'm not lying. He umm...I was upset. The day after the Halloween party and after we fought, I was still fuming about it. And when I left that morning and came back to the house and you still had an attitude and wouldn't let it go...it was a lot, okay. I was angry because you pissed me off—"

"I didn't piss you off."

The tone of Luke's voice changed. He was too calm all of a sudden, too...distant.

"What I did was ask you questions you didn't want to answer," he continued. "Questions that, apparently, you couldn't answer without incriminating yourself. So instead of telling me the truth then, you rushed to defense and anger." He looked at her, looked through her. "You pissed yourself off and then you left."

"Luke—"

"Did you leave here and go to him?"

Aris twisted her hands, her eyes pleading. "Yes."

"Did you fuck him?"

"No!" Aris took a few steps closer but stopped when he backed away from her. "No. I wouldn't do that."

He turned away, disgusted. "What *did* you do?"

After taking a few deep breaths, Aris finally found her words and confessed. "I needed to zone out, so I went over to his place to work."

"You left me and went to him."

"I went to work."

Luke shook his head, releasing a humorless laugh.

"Troy saw that I was upset and tried to get me to talk and after a while I started to vent. He listened and things kinda got weird and then he kissed me." She looked at him, her eyes pleading with him again to not believe the worst, to give her a chance to explain. "But I stopped it right away."

"You should've stopped it months ago."

Aris nodded, feeling defeated. "You're right. You're absolutely right and I'm sorry...so, so sorry. I didn't mean for any of this to happen. I didn't know—"

"You did know. You pretended not to, but you did."

"No, I..." Aris shook her head as fear gripped her. "I know I messed up, okay? Really bad, but I love you. You know that."

"You *say* that...and I swear I want to believe you because every time I hold you, every time we kiss, every time I'm inside you, I feel it." Luke ran a hand over his head, looking at her in bewilderment. "But then you allow shit like Troy to happen."

"It was a terrible mistake," she added desperately. "It was wrong and I'm so sorry. He crossed a line, violated our friendship—"

"All by himself?"

Aris frowned in confusion. "What?" She searched his face, saw herself in his eyes. "You can't possibly think that I would—"

"Why shouldn't I?" Luke gave her a critical once-over. She shrunk underneath his gaze. "Your mother died and that left you with one parent, one that didn't really learn how to show you love until this year. That type of hurt is foreign to me, so I can't even begin to imagine what that felt like, what that must have taught you...how you managed to survive it."

"Why are you bringing this up?" Aris asked, her voice painfully low. Tears threatened to slip and fall, but she lifted her chin and kept them at bay. "That's all in the past."

"You think so, huh? Funny...cause I don't. I think it's a part of you now."

It was her turn to turn away from him.

"Your father practically shut you out for the better part of a decade," Luke continued. "You don't move on from something like that. You find distractions."

"And your point is what?" Aris spat angrily. "To add daddy issues to my neverending list of faults?"

"It's not your fault."

"Ahhh, okay. So let me get this straight." She whirled around to face him, her eyes shining. "You're saying that I'm not to blame, but I do have issues because I'm harboring drama from childhood. Oh and I'm also a distraction-finder…add that to the list too, right?"

Luke stared at her. "Is that what I am to you," he finally asked. "Is that all that I've been for you… another fucking distraction?"

Aris's head jerked back like she'd been hit. Her anger slipped and, finally, so did the tears. "No. You know me. I fucking *love* you, Luke. *You know that.*"

"Do you? Are you even sure? Do you even know?"

She dropped her head and wiped her face with her hand before she looked up and met his gaze. "Yes. I do know and I am sure…but clearly, you're not." She took a deep, shaky breath and lifted her chin again. "If you're so unhappy with my past and who I am and the way I love you, then why are you even with me?"

"That's not what I said."

"Isn't it?" Her lips trembled and her eyes glistened, but still she refused to cry. "I know I'm fucked up, but I have done nothing but try to love you. I may not be perfect but neither are you, Luke Donovan, and, at very least, I have always accepted you for who you are and loved you anyway. And I still do, even after all your conclusions and attributions, even after you stand here, judging my past and reading me like a fucking case study. Well, love it or hate it…this is me." She stepped closer to him, shaking, barely able to contain her animosity. "So if who I am isn't good enough for you, then fuck you and fuck off."

"How you love is who you are, Aris," Luke replied calmly. "So, if you were me, based on what you've done…could you honestly say that's good enough?"

They stared at each other in silence until Luke cursed under his breath and backed away from her. There were a myriad of emotions she saw reflected in his eyes, but the one that broke through her anger and indignation and finally pierced her heart was the hurt.

She had hurt him.

To the point that he wasn't even looking at her the way he always had...and he probably never would again. The thought of that, of what she may have just lost, of what she'd inadvertently done, finally made her tears fall.

Aris couldn't move as Luke turned away from her, distancing himself even more. All she could feel was panic as he grabbed his keys and stormed out of their bedroom and, soon after, their house.

She wanted to call out to him.

She wanted to make him stop.

She wanted to take back everything she had done.

How you love is who you are.

For months, she'd dismissed his concerns as jealousy, insecurity and an incessant need to control.

But she hadn't been able to hear his heart.

She hadn't been able to assure him that he was nothing like Ralph, Marcel, Shane, David or the others, to assure him that he was so much more to her than they ever were.

And now it was too late.

Now, that one day she'd always feared had finally come and Luke was gone.

~ 24 ~

Kim listened while Aris cried.

They'd been on the phone for the past hour although not much had been said. There wasn't much to say at this point other than explaining how she'd officially hit a new low. Not so much because Aris was sobbing so hard she was barely able to form words, though it was a super huge factor, but more so because she'd had every possible opportunity to prevent the pain she was currently experiencing...but she hadn't. And the result was entirely on her.

"Luke loves you," Kim said when Aris calmed down enough to listen. "Just give him some time."

They hung up shortly after, but Aris knew that time was the last thing she wanted to give Luke because time wasn't on her side. It would work against her, allowing Luke the space to realize that he'd made a mistake moving in with her, being with her, loving her…that he was better off without her.

Aris stared at the phone in her hands. Without pause, she called Luke.

Voicemail.

She called him again and again and again.

Voicemail. Voicemail. Voicemail.

As the spaced tones filled her ear, she struggled with what to say after the beep and each message was full of nothing, which was apropos because it was exactly the way she felt.

After a final attempt, she stopped calling and yanked open the bottom drawer of her nightstand to remove a tattered, yellow folder crammed with small, significant strips of carefully written affirmations that was sure to fill the nothingness.

Tears fell again as Aris slowly thumbed through each one. It had been a while since she'd had to break open the folder, the last time being the day before she and Luke decided to share a house full time, since they committed to being more and doing more…together.

But now…it may all be over.

Needing a distraction, Aris stared at the phone in her hands. Fought her impulse. Struggled to not dig up what should stay buried, to not allow the lie to once again pose as the truth. So instead of the TALK button, she activated an app and crushed candy until her tears blurred her vision. The distressing emotions were deep, searing, shaming and debilitating in its pursuit to break her…but she allowed herself to feel all of it.

No jumping over it.

No running around it.

No crawling beneath it.

No getting away from it.

No shortcuts. No distractions.

Instead, Aris chose to go through it, chose to keep moving forward while being surrounded by an endless wall that was closing in quickly, chose to stay on the straight and narrow path that stretched out ahead of her as far as her spirit could see.

It was hell, but her blurry eyes stayed focused on her app while she played a game to ease the pain, clearing the jelly and bombing every obstacle in her way until she finally solved the puzzle.

Level up.

There were many more to go, but still…she won.

Tossing her phone aside, she grabbed a book from her nightstand. She'd discarded it weeks ago, but it was yet another welcomed distraction that eventually calmed her mind and cued her body to relax and finally…release.

~ 25 ~

Luke entered the house just before dawn, fully expecting Aris to be upstairs in bed, hoping that she was sound asleep. His plan was to grab some stuff and slip back out to avoid another confrontation.

He didn't want to see her.

He didn't want to fight her.

He didn't know *what* he wanted to do with her.

Luke was at a total loss for this realm of rage. It was foreign and forceful, and it scared the shit out of him.

When he entered the master bedroom, his eyes found Aris against his will causing his heart to physically hurt from just seeing her. Failing again to resist his urge to go to her, he soon found his way to her side of the bed. She was asleep just as he'd hoped with a book fanned open on her chest.

Needing to see her face, Luke clicked the tiny lamp on her nightstand and easily excused the dark streaks of mascara on her cheeks as a trick of the soft lighting before he looked closer and conceded to what he could only assume were too many shed tears.

Aris had been crying.

Or worse...she was crying in her sleep.

Luke's bitterness waned at that sudden realization and weakened even more when he noticed a well-worn, yellow folder that Aris must have tossed aside given that it lay open on the bed. He picked it up and read each strip of paper, one strip in particular that he quickly recognized as his words to her the night they first met. Aris had invited Luke inside her apartment after he'd given her a ride home from the sports bar where he happened to see her sitting alone at the bar. Later that same night—after she served him a burnt, thank-you breakfast—Luke learned that Aris's car had been seized thanks to her ex, Ralph Jones, who decided to play the part of an acrimonious Repo Man and left her stranded to prove yet another point in the power struggle that they deemed a relationship.

Luke's eyes traveled back to Aris, the woman he could not help but love but who frustrated him to no end. The woman he wanted to figure out so badly that he often talked with Tony and Celeste in hopes of stumbling upon some epiphany that he never would have expected to find inside the worn, yellow folder in his hands.

How had he never discovered it before?

They had been living under the same roof for months now and never once had he seen it. As Luke crossed the room to sit in the chair, he watched Aris as she slept, suddenly remembering a conversation he'd had with Celeste weeks ago. They spent an hour talking about how long it had taken Celeste to get Aris to open up, to trust her, to not be afraid to believe something that could destroy her if it ended up being a lie. It was a chat that occurred while Aris and Tony were sitting on the porch, a heart-to-heart that he hadn't expected. It surprised him to learn that Celeste was experiencing similar struggles with Tony.

She fully understood his plight.

With an admirable display of peace and patience, Celeste had reminded him to give Aris as much space as she needed and to forgive her when, not if, she stumbled. Celeste had been doing the same with Tony for months, giving him the grace to learn how to love and, over time, she had been rewarded with the love of her life.

"Never perfect," she said to him, laughing easily with a twinkle in her eyes. "but always genuine."

Luke placed the folder on the small table next to him and looked through the glass of the French doors.

Dawn was approaching.

His eyes found Aris again.

He had no idea how many more times this woman would break his heart.

But he did know that she loved him.

Pushing himself up from the chair, Luke removed his clothes and padded across the carpet. As soon as he stretched out in bed and pulled the covers over him, Aris did as she always did—unconsciously found his body and practically attached herself to him. He kissed her forehead and held her close, grinning because she hadn't awakened or moved once since he arrived home and entered their bedroom. The light from the lamp. The rustling of the yellow folder. None of it had bothered her at all.

Even now, after snuggling closer to him, Aris still hadn't roused from her deep slumber.

Lying on his back with Aris secure in his arms, Luke closed his eyes and focused on her even breathing until he was able to surrender the remaining remnants of his anger and finally succumb to his own peaceful sleep.

Luke woke to see Aris staring at him.

He raised a brow, wondering how long she'd been watching him. "You know that's creepy as hell, right?"

She gave him a shy smile before looking away.

She was anxious about something.

Instead of pressing her about it, Luke sat up and dropped his feet to the floor before leaving the bed for the bathroom. When he returned, she followed him back to bed with her eyes.

"You came back."

The fear in her eyes was unmistakable.

He eased closer to her, holding her gaze.

"I'll always come back."

Her shoulders visibly relaxed before she offered him another small, hesitant smile.

Luke waited for her to speak but the silence became too much. "Baby, what's—"

Aris pressed her finger to his lips before he could get a word out. "I was wrong."

Surprised by her words, Luke waited for more.

"I ended my friendship with Troy."

Luke tried not to smile at that, still waiting for more.

"I can also admit that I was projecting…or however you put it, my past issues onto you unfairly." She ran a hand over her hair, her eyes cast down. There was more silence as she paused, then she began again. "I'll never be perfect, but I will keep trying to be a great girlfriend for you…because you're worth it. And also because I truly want to do and be whatever you need whenever you need it so you can feel safe, comfortable, secure and whatever other mood you may be shifting through because it's my job to make you smile."

Grinning, Luke narrowed his eyes. "Haven't I heard this before?"

Aris wrinkled her nose. "Why you gotta go and bring up old shit?"

"My bad," he said, holding up his hands in mock surrender. "I'm trippin'. You got it."

"Damn right, Donovan." She leaned in to give him a sweet kiss. "And don't you forget it."

~ 26 ~

"Dammit. This is it." Aris grimaced and shut her eyes melodramatically. "This is how it ends..."

"You're about to die again?" With one arm around Aris, Luke extended his other to grab a frosty bottle from the end table. "Expiring in the bed might be a lot more comfortable, babe. Try that."

Aris cracked one eye open.

"Go get in the bed," he insisted after swallowing and placing the empty bottle back on the table. "I'll be there in a minute."

Rising from the sofa, Aris glared down at him. "I'll be sure to remember this the next time you need both your heads rubbed."

"What?" Luke asked innocently, his eyes glued to the new flat panel screen that he recently bought and had installed above the fireplace.

Aris was competing with Sunday Night Football.

She'd been resting in Luke's arms the entire game, watching his team play against a division rival, up three points with only two minutes left before the end of regulation. Just twenty-four hours ago, Aris was alive and well, eating and drinking to her heart's content at a popular Mexican restaurant for an after-work celebration. Last night had been good times with good people but now...she was on the brink of death.

"Whatever...I'll take care of myself," Aris mumbled as she slowly shuffled out of the family room.

"Baby, come on...I've been taking care of you since you stumbled in here last night," Luke said, finally tearing his eyes from the game to glance at her. "Just give me about ten more minutes, and I'll bring you a banana and some ginger ale."

Aris didn't respond. Instead, she swayed on her feet a bit and moaned for additional dramatic effect but it was a total waste because Luke's eyes were once again glued to his sixty-five inch prized possession because the defense allowed another first down with only 1:17 left to play.

She'd be invisible for at least another five minutes.

Her stomach tightened and rolled again.

She would die alone.

Aris shuffled along to their bedroom to bury herself underneath a soft and super-heavy patterned blanket that Luke brought back from his overseas trip two weeks ago. At first, she'd just looked at him when he presented the gift to her because...a blanket. Really? But now it had quickly become her brand new prized possession and, shockingly enough, the most luxurious addition to their bedroom décor.

After grabbing the remote from Luke's nightstand, Aris pressed the ON button to activate a much less stylish television that was perfectly positioned inside of a modernized, cherry-finished armoire against the wall across the room. As soon as the game appeared on screen, Luke's voice filled the house as the clock ran out and his team pulled out another win. She cheered with him in solidarity but not too much. Their home was a house divided, their respective teams predicted to match up at some point during the playoffs.

But not today.

Which is why Aris low-key celebrated with her man because any time an NFC team knocked out an AFC rival, it was a great day.

Just as she settled against a pile of propped pillows and cringed at the rumbling from her upset stomach, Luke appeared with a tray that held two bananas, a cup of apple sauce, a bowl of mashed potatoes, a can of ginger ale and a glass of water. She sat up and smiled as he set the tray on her lap. After placing his hand against her forehead, Luke felt her neck. Satisfied that her body wasn't too warm, he crossed the room to the armoire and loaded the DVD player and returned to strip down to his boxers and lay in bed with her.

"My team won," Luke shared as he grabbed another remote from the nightstand to switch the input source.

After taking a generous bite of her banana, Aris lifted her arms high above her head, signaling a touchdown. Luke grinned as she bounced around and then guided her to relax against him. When she noticed the opening credits of the movie he'd inserted into the DVD player, Aris cheered again.

Hope Floats.

Aris leaned over to slide the tray onto her nightstand, careful not to knock the lamp, phone or anything else over in the process. Once that task was completed, she shifted closer to Luke and tangled her limbs with his to watch the opening scenes of her favorite movie but was soon snoring softly in Luke's arms well before Birdee made her long, brave drive with her daughter back to her home town.

"Hey, let me run something by you."

Aris turned away from her latest mannequin and peered up at Luke who was waiting for her to give the green light. He rarely ever disturbed her while she was working, especially when she was in her zone. Aris didn't mind his presence now or ever, but Luke's respect for her craft and creative time was so solid and completely genuine that she accepted his consideration and left it up to him to decide when he wanted to hang out and watch her work. Lately, due to his work schedule, those times were few and far between, so the fact that he was interrupting now let her know that what he had to share must be pretty important.

"Shoot."

Luke sat on the sofa and leaned forward with his elbows on his knees. "I was wondering if you would like to take a vacation the day after Thanksgiving? I know that's a lot to ask given that we're already spending Monday through Thursday with my family in Savannah, but I think the timing is good with all these winter deals going on. I was thinking maybe we could take that whole next week off too...if you can manage the extra time off?"

"Yes."

Luke looked surprised at her affirmative response, probably because she'd uttered it so quickly. Not too long ago, she would've instantly hesitated and checked her upcoming schedule to share potential conflicts. Instead, she was wiggling on the floor in excitement.

Hell yeah, she would manage the extra time off.

Spending time with Luke was a no-brainer.

Especially after almost losing him.

After Aris and Luke found their way back to each other the morning after he walked out on her and almost gave up on their relationship for good, nothing else mattered to Aris except making sure that they would be always together. It took almost losing Luke for her to realize that a future with him didn't scare her as much as a future without him.

That was inconceivable.

"Good." Luke sat back against the sofa cushions. "Now, the next thing—"

Aris sighed and turned back to her mannequin. "Are you about to project manage me?"

Luke chuckled. "No baby...I just wanted to know if you would be cool with Tony and Celeste spending Thanksgiving in Savannah with us too?"

"For real?" Aris jerked her head and body around to face him again, her eyes wide. It was a great suggestion and one she had been thinking about pitching to Luke as well. She thought about her father's words, about them promising not to mess up the new family they now had with Luke and Celeste. "I think that would be perfect," Aris agreed with an animated shake of her head.

"Okay, I'll call your Dad tonight." He draped his arm over the back of the sofa and grinned. "And I'll hold off on us narrowing down vacation destinations since you feel like I'm *project managing* you…"

"You know I was just teasing about that…a little."

Luke grunted in amusement and then asked what cities she was interested in visiting. After traveling so much for the past year, Luke didn't really care where they ended up because he'd most likely already been. All that mattered to him was spending much-needed quality time with Aris, so wherever she chose would be more than fine with him.

"I was thinking," she said after they tossed around several cities. "Maybe we should do San Diego."

"Again?" he asked, remembering their trip there for Comic-Con last summer. "Plus, I thought you really wanted to do New York since you've never been?"

"I do, but we've plenty of time for New York," Aris clarified, trying to ignore his goofy grin at her subtle mention of their future together and fight her own smile. "We didn't get to stay very long and experience the city the way we should have…not to mention the weather is perfect…"

"Okay, baby. San Diego, it is."

"Yay." Aris bounced her shoulders before tilting her head all the way to the left and letting her body roll in a Matrix-style execution of the snake.

Luke laughed without comment and stretched out,

propping his head on a throw pillow to watch his girlfriend return to her mannequin to work her magic.

After about two hours, Aris lifted her arms above her head and groaned from having sat on the floor with no back support for such a long time. She rose to her feet in search of a toilet and Luke, the latter of which she found upstairs, stretched out again on the love seat in the sitting area of their bedroom. Watching some sports show, of course.

Aris smiled at his relaxed posture, happy that he wasn't hard at work in their office even though she'd been working for the past several hours herself. They were both trying to cut back on work and focus more on each other, and it was beyond amazing the overall impact it was having on their relationship in such a short time.

With her phone in hand, Aris strolled through the bedroom and into the bathroom to relieve her bladder and search for something fun to do now that her work was done. It had been almost a week since Luke had surprised her with their last impromptu date night and, now that it was her turn to initiate, she could wait to one-up him with her creativity. But her first order of business was to crush some more candy…

Because she was nothing if not competitive.

Commercial break.

Luke stood and headed for the bathroom.

After a few steps, he almost stopped in his tracks,

surprised to see that Aris left the door wide open. He fully expected it to be closed, as usual, and his plan had been to barge in and to annoy her, as usual.

Curious, Luke continued through the doorway and found Aris sitting on the toilet with the door to that small room open as well. She lifted her head at his presence, dismissing whatever she'd been doing on her phone. He waited for her to put him out as she always did but it never happened, prompting Luke to hike his brows and initiate a voiceless conversation.

So you're cool with me barging in now? his ask.

What does it look like to you? hers returned.

Luke watched in amusement as Aris twisted her lips and rolled her pretty eyes for emphasis before she lowered her gaze back to her cell phone. He turned to face the sink and wash his hands then looked up and caught his reflection. Shaking his hands dry, he moved to open the shower door and turn on the water spray, testing her benevolence. Then, he stripped and waited for Aris to finally yell for him to get out but she remained uncharacteristically silent, apparently too engrossed with whatever was happening on her phone to pay him any attention.

Stepping into the steaming shower, Luke grinned like a fool but he didn't care one bit. It felt good to get this point in their relationship...for Aris to finally and completely let her guard down with him and for them both to know and appreciate that they were together—a true couple—in every sense of the word.

Pleased by that welcomed revelation, Luke leaned back from the water spray to glance through the glass shower door. In this position, he had a perfect view of

Aris who was still on the toilet. She eventually felt his eyes on her and lifted her head to scowl and ice him out but her faux anger slipped into a grin before she shifted her eyes back down to her phone.

Luke laughed out loud and stepped back under the water spray, assuming she was probably playing her favorite puzzle game, still stuck on level 143. Three mornings ago, he woke up to discover her playing it in the dark, her sweet face screwed up because she couldn't clear all the jelly. It wasn't too long ago that Luke wouldn't have been caught dead wasting his time with such games but, with Aris, he simply rubbed his eyes and leaned over to stare at her phone in the dark with her, occasionally pointing his finger at the screen when she seemed to be stuck and unable to make the next move. After five attempts and five fails, Aris had thrown her phone at the bottom of the bed in protest. She was a supreme sore loser, but Luke hadn't allowed her to pout for long before he disappeared between the sheets to take her mind off the candy-crushing losses.

It always worked.

Smiling at the memory, Luke stepped out of the shower and wrapped a towel around his waist, making sure that Aris saw him drip-dry his way toward the bedroom. She laughed before he made it out of the bathroom, her eyes still focused on her phone while she sat on the toilet with the door *still open*…

Luke got the message.

Loud and clear.

Aris was finally all in…

And all his.

~ *Epilogue* ~
DECEMBER

"This is perfect."

Clad in a deep blue maxi skirt and a bikini top with a colorful drink in her right hand, Aris was reclined next to Luke and enjoying the spectacular beachfront view from the private patio of their residential-style cottage rental on Coronado Island. With its seaside charm and highly-personalized service, it was an outstanding way to experience sunny San Diego.

They were now in Day 3 of their one-week vacation and hadn't done much more than lounge around during the days and take advantage of their outdoor fire pit for the cool nights. Both were in recovery mode after a fun-filled holiday with the family in Savannah. From the moment they arrived at Luke's childhood home, it was a nonstop parade of family, friends, food and fun. Thanksgiving arrived with lots of sun and a cloudless sky, and everyone ditched the house to spill out into the massive backyard like it was the second coming of Labor Day weekend. Aris had enjoyed it all from her favorite spot with lots of pie and cobbler to keep her satisfied. For hours, she'd stuffed herself silly from what was the largest Thanksgiving spread she had ever seen while happily watching the festive, fifty-five family members and friends from a comfortable distance, still in awe that they now considered *her* family as well.

Luke had spent most of his time with his brother and cousins, sitting at a fold-up table drinking and playing spades. Celeste talked and laughed nonstop, becoming fast friends with Sarah Donovan and her sisters while Tony stayed seated a few feet away, appearing as overwhelmed by all the activity as Aris had been the very first time she was exposed to this blue-lights-in-the-basement-slash-sports-bowl-slash-cigar-bar-slash-black-Broadway-slash-comedy-jam-slash-independent-film-fest-slash-hip-hop-lounge-slash-kiddie-playhouse-slash-open-mic-night-slash-high-school-musical-slash-gospel-stage-play-slash-melting-pot come to life.

Even now, Aris laughed to herself at how her father had looked ready to bolt, completely surrounded by a mix of at least four of those categories. But, just as hers had, Tony's anxiety slowly began to fade. Luke's entire family was so genuine that you couldn't help but relax and go with the flow. It was their way.

"What's so funny?"

Aris turned her head to grin at Luke. "Just thinking about Thanksgiving. My dad had a really good time."

"I think good time might be pushing it, babe," Luke

replied with a laugh. "Glad they didn't scare him off though. It was touch and go for a while, but I think he finally found his footing once Uncle Joe got him talking. He's from a small family too, and it took him a while to adjust to us after he married my aunt Deb a few years ago." Luke laughed again. "By the end of the night, Tony and Joe looked like partners in crime."

"Shocked the hell out of me." Aris grinned. "I'm really glad they came. It was the best holiday I've had in like...ever. Can't wait to see what Christmas is like."

"Trust me, you can..." Luke shook his head. "It's a three-ring circus. If you can make it through that, you can make it through anything."

"I want to make it through everything."

Slipping his hand in hers, Luke grinned. "You better chill out with all that good talk before you end up back at that drive-thru chapel with me..."

Aris simply smiled and gazed out into the horizon.

"You would really go back to that chapel with me?" she finally asked.

"I most definitely would."

"Even after everything?"

Aris could feel Luke's eyes on her, but she kept looking straight ahead.

"We've had our challenges, yes," Luke finally said. "But I'm just as sure about you now as I was the night I drove you home after you nutted up in the parking lot of the sports bar when your car got jacked."

She frowned. "Why you bringing up old shit?"

Luke laughed. "My point is...I want you. No matter what we go through, I will always want you. And before you freak out like you did in Vegas, there's no pressure. Trust me, I'm not going anywhere...you are officially stuck with me. Plus, we've got plenty of time for all that stuff—marriage, babies, everything. Just know that anything that happens with us from here on out will be up to you, and I'll be ready for whatever, whenever and however...when you are. All you have to do is say the word."

Aris looked down at her hands and smiled. "You seriously think that I can make you happy for the rest of your life?"

"Nope."

At that, Aris looked at him and frowned.

"You're probably gonna piss me off and get on my nerves for the rest of my life...but at least I'll never be bored," Luke explained. "But that's okay. I don't want nor do I expect perfect, Moody. I prefer purpose, passion and peace...three things that no one else can provide me. Only you can."

"You seem pretty sure about me, Mr. Donovan."

"Like I already said...I've been sure since the moment I laid eyes on you, but I guess we had to go through what we went through to end up right here, right now."

Tilting her head, Aris stared at him in disbelief. "So even through all of our mess, you really believed that we would end up here?"

Luke pressed his forefinger against her forehead to smooth the wrinkled skin between her eyes. "I wasn't sure where or how we would end up, baby, but I was certain of one thing...that we would never be over."

Luke pulled her closer to his chest, and Aris gazed up into his eyes. "Damn, Donovan...you be knowin' for real." Impressed, she brushed her lips against his then paused to pull back and look into his eyes. "Oh, one more thing…"

His eyes narrowed. "What's that?"

Her lips stretched into a brilliant smile. "Word."

ACKNOWLEDGMENTS

Book 6…WOO! ☺ Again, I am humbled to have done this one more time. Lord, I give You praise.

I must say this book was a surprise. When I finished writing *Dawn of Aris*, the story of Aris and Luke felt complete to me and I was ready to move on…but then I heard back from a few readers who eventually helped me to change my mind about that. I wasn't always sure how the continuation of this story was going to unfold, but every time I was about to toss my laptop across the room in frustration, I remembered why I started…

Yvette, I can't thank you enough for your endless support and occasional nudges for me to stay on point…and finish this book! lol And special thanks to the first readers of *The Aris Effect*—Sharon, Shakir, Coty and yes, Yvette!—I truly appreciate each of you for encouraging and challenging me to be the best version of myself as I continue to push this pen. From my heart, THANK YOU! ♥ You are the real MVPs!

And to YOU, the reader—thank you so much for giving me a chance and spending this time with me. I am forever grateful. If this is your first time rocking with me, I invite you to visit raelamar.com where there are blog posts, excerpts, outtakes and sneak peaks of stories to come. Leave me a message and/or connect with me on social media...either way, I'd love to hear from you. Also, I welcome your comments about *The Aris Effect* so please share your thoughts by posting a review and/or rating on Amazon or Goodreads. Your feedback matters!

Now, back to writing.

Until next time...

Peace and Blessings,

RL

About the Author

Rae Lamar is a mild-mannered consultant by day and fiction writer by night who calls Atlanta home. She is also author of *DAWN OF ARIS*, *22*, *UNLIKE ME*, *SOMEWHERE IN BETWEEN* and *OPEN*. To learn more about Rae, visit raelamar.com.

www.ingramcontent.com/pod-product-compliance
Lightning Source LLC
Chambersburg PA
CBHW050028180626
46810CB00002B/631